SLICE

A SHORT STORY

It seemed he had nothing to lose and everything to gain.

Half orphaned and struggling to survive,
he didn't doubt he could save his family with a power enhancing drug.

by
Drew Briney

D1418264

1 片

Tzun quickly rounded the corner, discretely dropping the wallet he'd just lifted from an inattentive merchant and nimbly feathering his fingers through a thick set of freshly printed bills. *That should be enough for an entire week ... or more,* he congratulated himself. That, of course, would depend on which numbers were written on the bills and how wisely he used them – but these details were of little consequence. This was a game of survival. Then again, in tough times, it seemed like everything was about survival.

Short and somewhat scrawny, Tzun had some difficulty in quickly making it to his destination without drawing attention to himself by running. A brisk walk was all he could discretely afford. Two more buildings and he could pass through the alleyway to Mariner's Market Street where he would quickly disappear in a crowd. Dressed in beggarly clothes, eyes would naturally divert themselves away from the gaunt, young, half asian rather than retrace his visage for a second glance. From there, he would only be a few blocks from his modest apartment where he lived with his mother and extended family. This morning's prize would be well received.

But fate couldn't bear to smother Tzun in blankets of kindness for too long.

Before he turned the next corner into the alleyway, muffled screams covered by scuffling and hushed chuckling teased the air. *Blasted fate!* He didn't need any trouble – but it was coming nonetheless. Primordial instincts from deep within screamed to his consciousness that something wasn't right – beyond the apparent crime, something felt out of place – but he couldn't put his finger on it.

Four young men who clearly devoted more time building muscles rather than character gathered around some dainty brunette, a young girl who almost looked too innocent to have set foot in this neighborhood. *Bloody bricks!* Tzun silently cursed, considering this new dynamic and quickly absorbing every new detail of this ever-changing pathway. The dumpster was farther away from the west wall than normal. A hubcap lay at an angle, leaning next to that same wall. A small box of screws lay spilled near the feet of two of the larger boys – one of whom was holding the girl; two stacked boxes of junk appeared undisturbed since he had seen them there earlier that morning; the antique chair that had been next to the dumpster now sported a broken leg and the upholstery was looser near the top of the leg stump. Other than these few details, the alleyway looked precisely the same as it had a few hours earlier.

Behind Tzun, footsteps approached but slowed; hesitant, they either stopped or became silent. Above those feet, a hand brushed aside an over-length jacket and placed a recently discarded wallet into a back pocket.

If he played his cards well, Tzun estimated that he could divert his eyes to the left, walk along the other side of the alleyway, and then freely pass by unharmed – the thugs would leave him alone. He posed no threat to their fun and they would presume verbal threats would keep him from reporting anything to the police. Then, the distraction would be over. To them, Tzun would be nothing more than a lanky sixteen year old beggar, unworthy of their attention.

But he was *Uzzit* so he couldn't in good conscience do nothing.

Shoving the stash of money deeper into his pocket and underneath a fold designed to hide prize lifts from family members when necessary, Tzun stopped walking, stood as erect and intimidating as his thin five-foot-nine frame could muster, slowly raised his head, and ordered the thugs to release the girl in the most threatening voice he could muster. Despite his best efforts, the inevitable unwelcomed response came as expected: they chortled and then laughed openly.

It always went down like this.

Carefully observing the spilled screws and the lone hubcap, Tzun focused his thoughts on the weather, creating a quick gust of wind to cover his Uzzit magic. As he knelt down to pick up a chunk of junk metal from the ground next to his feet, he sent the hubcap shooting into the lead thug's ankle, a volley of dust into the eyes of another boy, and the box of screws into the neck and face of another. For the boy holding the girl, Tzun sent a vivid hallucination that acid had splattered all over his body; fierce burning sensations turned to panic as the thug watched his own skin melting away. When his grip loosened from shock, the girl shook herself loose and bolted. Tzun threw the chunk of metal at her captor just long enough to give her the head start she needed. Although the metal hit its target, Tzun's efforts might as well have come from an eight year old girl unaccustomed to throwing balls – it didn't do much anything. For that matter, none of the attacks caused any significant damage – even the screws did little more than scratch the thug's face – but they did create the distraction needed to save the girl. Now it was his turn.

Quicker than anyone expected, Tzun was darting behind the dumpster, hoping to make his own escape. But from his limited perspective, he failed to notice one changed detail down the alleyway: entirely hidden in the shadows, two large antique batteries were resting against the wall on the other side of the dumpster. Tripping over them, Tzun stumbled heavily and just long enough to keep him from moving around the couch he knew would be resting by the wall on that same side. One stumble led to another until Tzun found himself face down and ungracefully sprawled over the ground. A moment later, vicious kicks repeatedly pounded his side and at least two blows connected with his head, leaving his ears ringing and his vision cloudy.

That wasn't quite how he planned things.

He thought he heard a whistle but wasn't sure. And then, that familiar feeling returned: something wasn't quite right.

Four sets of footsteps hurriedly ran down the alley away from Mariner's Market Street while another softer set methodically plodded towards Tzun. Propping himself up on one elbow, Tzun strained to open his eye to see what new trouble might be coming his direction only to discover that his eye was throbbing and that he couldn't see much of anything just yet. He reached up to touch it and winced at the pain. Somewhere, in the midst of that scuffle, he'd received a blow to his eye that he hadn't immediately noticed – but he certainly felt it now. Turning his head further, he opened his other eye to find a rough looking but clean cut fellow reaching his hand out to lift him up.

From boots to a hat that covered any hair that wasn't freshly buzzed, leather trappings of every sort decorated the newcomer. If he wasn't nearly bald, you couldn't tell so long as that hat was on. And as he softly smiled, he held one eye slightly squinted – as if it had to squint because of an unpleasantly large scar that reached from the middle of his bottom eyelid and through his hairline where it passed over a piece of missing ear – neatly sliced off in a fairly straight line. Further markings on this man's face betrayed some serious time on the streets. He looked downright rugged.

"That's quite a talent you have," he offered as he helped Tzun back to his feet.

Still dizzy and trying to keep his body from visibly trembling, Tzun struggled to retain his footing for a moment before responding. "Talent?" he feigned in ignorance.

"You're Uzzit aren't you kid?" The rough tone of voice left Tzun uncertain whether or not a question had been asked.

"The wind …" he began.

"Don't feed me that bull," the street warrior interrupted with an overly confident air. "I know Uzzit when I see it." His rigid gaze carefully scanned over Tzun who still looked more than a little dazed and worse for the wear, a boy who barely belongs on the streets, a boy who was lucky enough to have made it this far. And looks weren't deceiving. If Tzun hadn't been Uzzit, he would have been dead months ago – and he was acutely aware of this fact.

"How would you like to *really* grow in your powers?"

So that was it.

It had all been a set up. It made sense now. Girls that looked that innocent knew better than to walk this area alone. Women who frequented these parts of town looked much rougher for the wear than that girl. And the muscle-bound boys were chosen to exaggerate the mismatch. This had all been an effort to poach new Uzzit flesh – which meant the rumors were true. There really were drug dealing opportunists out there peddling their wares to this new generation of special kids.

"You have Slice?" Tzun tentatively queried.

"You've heard of it?"

"Who hasn't?"

"Answer my question first," the drug dealer ordered. "How would you like to double your powers?"

"Who wouldn't?" Brown, half Asian eyes blankly stared back at the older man.

"It comes with a price you know?" His worn face looked more hardened now as he looked down at this new, potential client.

"Yeah, I know," Tzun responded emotionless. *Bricks*! he swore to himself, rubbing his eye. It really hurt. "So what are the terms – and who's gonna teach me?"

"Today's price is whatever is in your pockets. Tomorrow's price is negotiable – and I'm your teacher." Then, with overt pretentiousness, the man pushed one finger forward and drew it downwards as if writing on the wall. As he did so, a bend and then a tear appeared at the top edge of the dumpster and continued until his finger stopped moving. The sound was deafening and gave Tzun another reason to hold onto his head. It seemed his eye injury was quickly becoming a headache.

"That must make you Max," Tzun responded, still holding his hands over his ears even though it was too late for them to do any good. He said nothing to indicate he was impressed but his good eye emphatically told that story. Max was legendary on the streets but no one ever got to meet him … When Tzun's instincts told him something wasn't as it seemed, they weren't kidding …

"Alright kid, what's in your pockets?"

The question left Tzun a little frustrated. On the one hand, this would be worth every bill he had lifted earlier that morning. On the other hand, he believed it unwise to play his cards openly. Convincingly feigning stiffness in his right arm, he dug his hand deep into his right pocket and deftly pulled three bills out of the hidden pocket, reclosed it, and produced them for inspection – all without causing the slightest suspicion that he was holding something back. To their common surprise, all three bills were large ones.

Crap! Tzun silently groaned with disappointment. *I should have pulled bills from the other end of the fold ...* "I just got a lucky lift," he explained. "I don't usually have that much," he added as he opened his pockets to show they were empty. The secret fold remained hidden.

"No problem kid," Max assured him, eyeing the cash with feigned indifference. "I won't expect that much every day. So you know the rules right? After three weeks, whatever Slice does to you becomes permanent. You miss a day, you have to start over and you might lose some of what you had before. And no cops right? Buying Slice is illegal; using it is illegal; making it is illegal. You get caught, you're going to the slammer for longer than I'll be around and the instant you get caught, old Max here will have zero memory of who you are or what you may have done. This is dangerous business kid. Got it? You still in?" Like most guys in the business, it never really seemed like Max was asking a question. It seemed more like he was saying: this is a done deal but if I have to do more fast talking to make this happen, I'll keep my mouth moving until you give in from exhaustion. Inevitably, the result would be the same.

Tzun feigned indecision for a moment, giving himself time to think over the consequences of what he was doing here. There really was no question though – he just needed to double check his resolve. What boy – especially a scrawny teenager worn from regular beatings – wouldn't take a three week ride to becoming a near superhero? Who doesn't want to be thrown away from their current life and into something bigger, better, happier? Who doesn't want more control over what is going on around them? For a thin teenage boy struggling to find his next meal, there really was no viable alternative – at least, Tzun didn't see any.

"Yeah, I'm in," he answered with cold determination.

"Aaaallright!" Max chuckled in response, stashing Tzun's prize cash into one pocket while reaching into another inside jacket pocket – all the while, a big smile spreading over his teeth. "Here's your package. This is enough for *two* days but I expect you to be here again tomorrow. You keep the extra dose just in case something bad happens some day and one of us is late to our meeting. Every day, we meet right here at this same time. Got it?"

"Got it." Tzun reached for the metallic brown liquid as he carefully noted the time on Max's watch. Tzun, of course, wasn't wearing one.

The young boy shuffled nervously as he slowly placed the vial in his right pocket and considered what he was doing. He felt better when Max tipped his hat, nodded, and walked away in the same direction as the other thugs had gone. It passingly occurred to Tzun that Max may have ordered the beating he had just received – but he was too naïve to seriously consider such a thing so the thought promptly dissipated. Besides, there were more important things to consider: if Tzun could hone his pickpocketing skills, he would quickly rise to the top of the food chain in three short weeks. If not ... well ... he wasn't going to think about that. He was already scrounging about the lowest levels of society – how much worse could it get?

He swirled the bottle and watched the liquid shimmer and change shapes as two separate hues emerged among the cloudy swirls. When he held the bottle still, the liquid quickly settled into a more uniform consistency. As he pondered over the opportunities Slice might present to him, Tzun began walking down the alley with an uncharacteristic spring to his step and then checked it; beggars couldn't appear too happy –

that would blow his cover. Modifying his gait, he considered various rumors he heard about Slice: it only worked on Uzzit. If it didn't kill normal people, they wished it had. But for people like Tzun, it unleashed access to those inner workings of the brain that scientists had been attempting to tap for decades.

If research in this field hadn't been heavily regulated and ultimately banned by nearly every industrialized country, Uzzit advancements would have been the global norm. American Uzzits were subjected of federal government regulations and inefficient bureaucracy, which led many of them to congregate in the Puget Sound area where government oversight and corruption allowed a quiet underground to steadily grow. Numbers of Uzzit were unknown. Uzzit births were unknown; undetectable without expensive testing, parents of Uzzit children were often unaware of their children's abilities for several years – but very few kept it secret as long as Tzun. His weak powers offered an element of surprise that he frequently needed to escape trouble but they did little to attract attention.

In the states, Uzzit enhancement drugs were controversial and experimental. On the black market, experimental versions of Slice could be purchased but resources were low and word had it that Max personally delivered every shipment of Slice, beating down every sign of potential competition. He never accepted solicitations and he always handpicked his clients. That made for stiff competition, high prices, and enduring loyalty that couldn't be bought in any other way. By some stroke of luck, Tzun was rising through that system. Life would never be the same.

His fingers instinctively wrapped around the cool vial, smothering it with tenacious attention. Passingly, Tzun considered that he didn't know how to divide the vial into two equal proportions – or perhaps that didn't matter. He could start out with a smaller portion this evening – surely that wouldn't matter for the first day? Not thinking about it, Tzun wiped some sweat off his brow and bumped his swollen eye.

As he winced, he considered that he could use his misfortune to his advantage.

Feigning a slight limp that increased as he moved along, he found a small opening on the boardwalk where many people were passing by, gingerly sat down, and began to beg for money. Deliberately rubbing his temples to temper the pain, he tilted his head to accentuate the injury to passersby. Fickle fortune returned as his companion for a few hours when his success became difficult to hide – his pockets were subtly bulging with money. Each time he received cash, he slipped larger bills into his hidden pocket and left smaller bills in the regular pocket. He happily considered that he probably had enough money for a few day's worth of Slice by the time he went home for supper.

"Hey," a soft voice called Tzun to look up. His bad eye nearly swollen shut, Tzun awkwardly turned his head to look upon the most beautiful face he had ever seen. In her twenties, dressed like she didn't belong in the area, and conspicuously attached to some burly fellow Tzun ignored, the young woman looked perfect in every way – except for the severely deformed and mangled hand that she used to pass on a substantial wad of bills to the young beggar. "Better times are coming," she encouraged with a sultry voice that left Tzun melting ... and then flushing in shame as she strolled away to purchase local wares.

Daily – if not more frequently – Tzun recycled rationales to justify his lifestyle. Uneducated, somewhat fatherless, and stuck in a crime infested town, he only did what familial obligations required: he begged and stole so his family could eat. But he refused to think of himself as a thief; *at least*, he periodically pontificated, *it isn't wrong to be a thief as long as you have good reasons to steal*. The fact that countless others used this same reasoning fortified his feelings of justification in what he did but something deeply embedded in his subconscious nagged at him to reconsider his life's path - so he regularly chanted this mantra to keep himself steady on the course he was following. And while he often lifted enough money to take care of his family, it never seemed quite enough and occasionally, extra money was needed to bail someone out of jail. Retracing his thoughts, Tzun watched his most recent benefactor as she meandered farther away from him. *People with enough money can buy stuff to regrow hands like that,* he considered. But she gave money to Tzun instead. Of course he felt ashamed – who wouldn't? Another stranger discretely gave Tzun a small offering as he passed by while Tzun drooped his head further, nearly pinning it between his knees.

As the hours passed and street life slowed down for the dinner hour, Tzun slowly stood up and slithered down the boardwalk, unnoticed by anyone at all. If he had any real talent, this was it: he could disappear – masterfully well. His right hand, now familiar with the vial it had been stroking throughout the day, held firm to its package. He needed to go somewhere private to divide his daily dose and see how it affected him. As he had thought about this while begging, he determined he would first go home, make his daily presentation of financial offerings to his family, visit the bathroom where he could hide his stash of money, divide the vial of Slice with a toothpaste cap, drink his daily dose, and go for a walk to the park where he could sit underneath some bushes and … experiment. He waited to take his first dose so he would have a strong buffer time between his meetings with Max. One missed day could lead to disastrous consequences – and that was a risk he wouldn't take.

Soon, Tzun was climbing the stairs to the second floor where his family lived. Part of him didn't want to go home today – his swollen (probably black) eye would be embarrassing and he would have to tell the same story half a dozen times to half a dozen family members before the night was over. The other part of him was thrilled and excited – how would Slice enhance his powers? Rumor had it that Slice was somewhat unpredictable: its effect on some people was minimal while its effect on others was nigh unto disastrous. But for most people, Slice just magnified the abilities of whoever was using it. Of course, Tzun knew he was taking a gamble by hoping that Slice would treat him well but he suppressed those considerations.

Hand held up to the doorknob, he briefly considered not opening the door to his apartment. What if he just downed half the vial right now, walked to the park, and learned what was going to happen without any further waiting? Maybe it would heal his eye – rumor said that Slice made some people heal ridiculously fast – but then, Tzun heard that from Patty and everyone knew she couldn't reliably regurgitate the truth. Or maybe Slice would enhance his psionic talents and allow him to control his Uncle Kan – the scariest relative in his family. To date, Tzun hadn't shared his Uzzit talents with anyone – not even with Koemi – so no one would suspect his taking control over Kan's mind for a while …

Without thinking, Tzun turned the knob, hung his head low, and brooded his way into the living room. With his bruised eye swollen shut, feigning depression would be easy and Kan probably wouldn't badger him for his share of the money as intensely as usual. Marie, his mother was the first to notice, then Aki, his aunt, then Ba Tu, his mentally handicapped father, and then a slew of cousins all together. Within ten minutes, the entire household was in its traditional uproar and given the situation, it was easy for Tzun to excuse himself into the bathroom for a few minutes while the women of the family returned to their traditional meal preparations.

Hand shaking, breath constricted, and pulse quickening, Tzun shut the door, locked it, unscrewed the toothpaste cap, pulled out the vial, popped off the cork top, and carefully measured slightly less than one half of the metallic liquid one portion at a time. Although gritty, Slice tasted somewhat like old car keys. And beyond that distinct metal taste, it sent subtle shocks of electricity down his tongue and throat, sort of like chewing tinfoil except that the tingling sensation traveled with the liquid all of the way down into the stomach. Almost immediately, Tzun felt energized and found himself hungrily sipping every last spec of Slice out of the toothpaste cap, carefully rinsing the cap with a couple drops of water, and sucking hard to make sure there was no Slice left in the cap. Leaving residue in the cap could be quite dangerous to other family members but Tzun nearly forgot to think about that. If anything, he felt strongly tempted just to drink the second portion of Slice and then come up with some lame excuse as to how he had spilt it on the ground so that he could get an extra serving – it was exhilarating, fulfilling, and demanding all at once – and Tzun soon felt growing impulses to do things he had never done before.

The next hour with his family was painfully unfulfilling – like how a child feels when promised ice cream on a road trip: the excitement only lasts so long before the wait becomes agonizing. In between explaining what had happened in the alleyway (conveniently omitting anything involving Max) and presenting a disappointingly paltry financial offering for the day, Tzun found himself largely distracted by things that were happening outside.

Juan, known for blaring his mariachi music louder than anyone else in the neighborhood cared to hear began a long volley of expletives when his radio sparked and popped until it failed to work entirely. Experimenting further, Tzun brushed Juan's mind with strong suggestions to include a string of defamatory rantings about his wife while banging on the radio – bringing no small fury from her tongue as she overheard what he had to say. A homeless dog known for random acts of aggression whimpered loudly and ran away down the alley. A short while later, a neighborhood bully sincerely and profusely professed his love to a stairwell while onlookers softly chuckled with eyebrows cocked and heads shaking. Other random incidents followed every few minutes.

Psionics were Tzun's passion but before today, he had only been able to master some few useful tricks. Even then, after a few bursts of effort, he usually felt drained and unable to do much anything else. Today was different. Tzun was embarking upon a new world. New ideas came readily and Slice opened his mind to make new efforts intuitive – instinctual. After an hour of experimenting and messing around with people's heads as they walked along the road below, Tzun felt like he was just warming up. The moment dinner was over, he nearly bolted out the door and went for that long awaited walk to the park.

2 片

"Kan, you really should teach him how to fight. Didn't you see his eye?" Marie coaxed, offering a prodigious puppy dog face to emphasize her point.

"Not a chance. You heard how he lost his temper and beat those boys last year."

"Oh come on, you know Koemi is prone to exaggeration. Look at Tzun's eye when he comes back. I really doubt her story carries much weight …"

"The boy talks to himself late at night, comes and goes at random times, and has no job. He must first learn discipline, to control his passions …"

"Kan," Marie interrupted in turn. *You're such a hypocrite.* "You began teaching your children before *they* were old enough to know these things. I know Tzun's Australian mother unforgivably gave him a Chinese name but he is still your family. You cannot expect him to survive these streets much longer at his size without some training. How much longer until …"

"No."

"Ba Tu would teach him but since his injury …"

"No."

"Kan …"

"No," Tzun's uncle repeated with exasperation. "He is already too dangerous. Koemi said that *two* of those boys last year went to the hospital in critical condition."

"Not true…" she sing-songed in response, trying to

retain her composure – and her patience.

"Why he let someone get the better of him again today, I don't know but I am certain of this …" he paused for dramatic effect, shaking his finger with frustration. "Tzun is a danger to those around him. He is constantly in fights, he is unstable …"

"He's a cheerful puppy dog who couldn't harm a spring chick," Marie interjected with unbelieving desperation, "he …"

"I will not take part in teaching him anything that will harm others. It is already shameful enough that he makes money stealing and begging. He …"

"Kan!" Marie interrupted. "Be reasonable. The boy has no means of getting a job – you yourself turned him down for a job – and surely you know *your own* children beg and steal to survive …"

Kan yelled something unintelligible and stormed off into the other room, knocking chairs aside and swearing words in Japanese that even Marie wasn't familiar with.

Being the Australian wife of a severely handicapped husband was rarely easy. Being dependent upon the mercies of a quasi-traditional, quasi-dysfunctional Japanese family was even worse. She enjoyed Asian cultures but this family seemed to have forgotten its heritage altogether. *Hypocrite,* she all but screamed in her own mind as she watched him leave. *Uuuooohh,* she silently grunted. *You couldn't at least teach him some self defense?* she sarcastically complained. Reasoning with Kan was as profitable as betting on race turtles but motherly instinct had required the attempt. Then again, Marie tacitly understood that Kan only allowed her and her crippled husband to stay so he could publicly protect his honor. The time would come when Kan would look for a good excuse to kick Marie, Ba Tu, and Tzun out of the house so she had to be careful not to push issues too hard. At the same time, it was becoming unbearably difficult to watch Tzun continually take beatings while roaming the streets just so he could put food on the table for her. The whole situation was one continual vicious cycle and she didn't know how to get out of it.

3 片

Bursting with energy, Tzun nearly felt out of control. He tried focusing his mind on healing his eye but nothing happened. He tried to make his muscles stronger so that he could run faster or jump higher. Nothing happened. Tzun saw a nerdy kid on the street corner trying to impress a blond girl way out of his league. She smugly walked over to the boy as if she were going to give him a major tongue lashing and instead … kissed him. He saw a little toddler on the corner staring wistfully at the only real flower garden in the entire city. Tzun sent her visual images of flowers dancing all around her and singing happy songs. The girl clapped in delight and called to her mother to show her the dancing flowers. Tzun tried to break a twig with his mind. Nothing happened. He used his mind to roll a small boulder a good ten feet. It worked. After messing around with several more random psionic tricks, Tzun began to feel physically drained and while he walked towards his apartment, he began to drag his feet as he awkwardly swaggered.

He didn't make it out of the park before passing out.

He woke up late the next morning and looked at an antique clock erected on a stone pillar at the south edge of the park. It was nearly time to meet Max. *Blasted bricks!* he swore at himself. *I have to hurry.* But as he tried to stand up, Tzun found himself unable to balance well on his feet and fell over twice before gaining enough control over his body to tentatively walk towards the alleyway where he had met Max. Nausea; fatigue; headaches; dizziness; sore muscles; they consumed him but he pressed on. Although only twenty minutes passed, Tzun felt as if he had heroically pressed through days of trials just to make it back into the alleyway. By the time he rounded the corner to meet Max, he worried that he might pass out while receiving his first Uzzit lesson.

Familiar leather trappings identified Max as the first man Tzun saw in the alleyway but there was another young man there, perhaps twenty years of age. His natural hair color was dubious underneath a strong coating of aqua coloring but Tzun guessed the man was naturally blond. A string of cursings poured out of his mouth as he argued with Max but the veteran drug smuggler barely responded. Instead, he simply hushed the younger man, brushed him aside with a cursory wave of his hand, and tossed a small package into the air. The man with aqua hair held onto whatever he caught like a starving man in a desert holds onto a diminishing flask of water and then ran around the corner as quickly as he could. The exchange left Tzun feeling uneasy as Max turned around.

"Hey kid, you made it!" Max said pleasantly as if nothing negative had happened in his life for days. "You never told me your name."

"Tzun."

"Soon?" he responded, puzzled.

"Ttttzzzun," the young boy repeated. "You hold your tongue as if you are going to say something that starts with a 'T' and then say 'Z' instead." The explanation wasn't quite right but it gave Americans a good shot at pronouncing his name.

"Got it … Tzun," Max repeated carefully. "You look awful kid. You didn't sleep well?"

"Uhhh, I don't know," Tzun confessed. "I sort of passed out on the way home last night."

"Oh. You didn't use Slice in the evening did you? I gave it to you yesterday morning – you should always use it before the afternoon."

"Oh," Tzun mumbled, feeling stupid even though no one had ever told him that before.

"No matter kid. Here, take a little extra now and then drink another dose after our lesson and you should start feeling better right away." Max threw a small vial at Tzun who wolfed down the liquid without a thought. Immediately, that tingling sensation buzzed down his throat and into his stomach as Slice made its way through his body. Then, Tzun's headache, soreness, and dizziness gave way to an exhilarating surge of energy. Even though it was only a small dose, he was entirely overwhelmed by the feeling it gave him. Max glowed with satisfaction as he observed the change in his client.

"Okay Tzun, how much money did you bring me today?"

Tzun pulled out a few small bills he kept in his pockets as a reserve in case he needed to buy food on the streets and briefly touched the only large bill he left stashed away in his hidden pocket. The rest of yesterday's earnings were hoarded away back home, underneath the bathroom counter and in a small bag where he kept his toothbrush, razor, and other personal hygiene items. He had sewn a secret compartment at the bottom of that bag so no one would find it and it came in handy from time to time.

"Here," Tzun offered the small stash of bills as if he was pleased with how much money he was giving Max. He suspected Max might not be satisfied with this paltry offering so he feigned pride so that, on the off chance Max objected, he could tell Max to count the money. Then, if Max was still unhappy, Tzun could say he had counted wrong and let Max count the money again before pulling out the larger bill from his hidden pocket. If Max said nothing, Tzun would say nothing.

"Really kid, that's it?"

Fairly relaxed and confident, Tzun feigned surprise. "Count it," he coaxed, "that's more than I can usually lift in three days," he claimed, only stretching the truth a little. The amount was more than he got to keep for himself after three day's lifting. Max counted the money.

"Alright," he conceded grumpily as he stashed the money in his pockets and pulled out a vial of Slice for Tzun to drink. "Don't drink that until after our lesson," he instructed, "but you need to drink it right away after we're finished. Got it?"

"Got it," Tzun repeated. *This guy's a drill sergeant,* he silently groaned. "What's our lesson today?" he pressed, brimming with hope.

"First off, I'm gonna need more money than that from day to day," Max complained. "Slice is expensive to make you know? I'll go broke trying to help people out if I can't at least pay for the production of your daily dose. Right? You follow me?"

"I'm following you," Tzun repeated. At least he didn't need to pay any extra money today but quickly calculating in his mind, Tzun estimated that his stash wasn't going to cover as much Slice as he'd hoped.

"Okay then, let's see you lift something," Max instructed.

Tzun nervously looked around him. There was no one in sight and he had never let anyone watch him pickpocket before. What if Max caught Tzun on video? "Ummm. You want to follow me to Mariner's Market Street?" he tentatively asked.

"Ha!" Max laughed with one of those hearty smoker's laughs that almost sounded more like a cough than a laugh. "No kid, I mean lift something; pick it up using your mind." He pointed to his head.

"Oh, gotcha," Tzun answered, feeling stupid again. Fortunately though, he had already thought through this part of the lesson. If he started big, Max might give him better lessons. If he started small, Max might later become impressed with his progress and be easier on him if Tzun ended up a little short on money. Street savvy in some ways, Tzun nevertheless sported a strong naïve streak so he opted for the possibility of better lessons – without even considering that Max might not be invested in these lessons or considering that the lessons were really just a means of keeping kids on Slice.

Bearing in mind that Slice enhanced his capabilities, Tzun gave everything he had to lift up one side of the dumpster, an object much larger than anything he had ever tried to move before – including the small boulder he rolled the night before. It moved but the one side of the dumpster didn't stay in the air very long before the wheels on the other side started rolling, ruining Tzun's control over it. It slammed back down onto the ground. Frustrated and initially too intimidated to look at his mentor, Tzun was slow to meet Max's gaze. He struggled to discern his mentor's reaction. Was he disappointed? Impressed? Was that surprise in his eyes? Tzun couldn't tell.

"Not bad kid," Max started, pursing his lips into a frown and bobbing his head up and down as if he was trying to be encouraging. "Do it again."

Those three words scared Tzun interminably. He desparately wanted to impress Max. He wanted a great lesson. He wanted direction. But he didn't think he could do it again. Levitation was Tzun's weakest Uzzit talent. Tzun focused. He tried to channel the energy he had received from the small dose of Slice he drank earlier but it felt almost used up and his strength was notably weakening. Remembering how Max had torn that same dumpster the day before, Tzun pushed his hand into the air as if he were going to lift the dumpster with his own hand. He pushed with his mind as well and tried as hard as he could to tip that dumpster over.

And it actually worked.

But the instant Tzun began to smile with satisfaction, he collapsed and his world went dark. Unhallowed visions enveloped him. Scenes as if from a horror movie flashed through his mind and tormented his body. Imprisoned in unconsciousness, Tzun learned depths of fear previously unknown to him. Even the venomous battling of street life held no candle to the haunting fears he suffered within the confines of his own mind. Suffocating and struggling to breathe throughout his hallucinations, the young boy lashed out at unseen attackers and silently screamed for help. His words were never heard, his sentiments never understood. He felt smothered. He felt as if he was falling. Perhaps this was the feeling of death.

Then, the taste of metal on his lips rushed through his subconscious thoughts, reviving him somewhat. Instinctively, his mouth opened wide, hoping to receive more medicine. Tzun coughed as a few drops of Slice trickled down his throat and into the wrong pipe. Sitting up in panic, he instinctively tried to recover the small splashes of the drug that escaped his mouth. He quickly spotted a trace of Slice on the back of his hand and a bead of Slice on his pant leg. Without thinking, he licked the back of his hand and wetting his finger, wiped every last speck of Slice from his clothing that he could find. Only after he finished cleaning up the spills did he notice that Max was holding the rest of Tzun's daily dose in front of him. He guzzled it down and sucked hard on the bottle to make sure he got every tiny metallic droplet into his system.

Max eyed him carefully. "Maybe Slice isn't good for you kid. You're taking this pretty hard." Then, after a pregnant pause, he asked a pointed question: "Do you have any other Uzzit in your family?"

"I'm it," Tzun answered truthfully.

"Really?" Max asked in disbelief, perhaps hoping for more clients or talented siblings.

"My dad was badly crippled when I was little. He can't do much," Tzun explained, "and I'm an only child." He didn't like questions about his family but his head was too cloudy to think through what he was saying. That was probably more personal information than he'd shared with anyone else for months.

"Uzzit traits are polygenic but it seems to be passed on through the moms," Max incorrectly explained. "Do you have any *step* brothers or sisters?"

"No," Tzun answered again.

"Too bad," Max interrupted. "It's always nice to have siblings … At any rate, this stuff is tough on you kid. Slice is unpredictable you know? It's better for some people than others. Maybe you should just let it go." With that, Max tipped his hat as he casually turned around and started walking down the alleyway as he had the day before.

"No!" Tzun countered, more aggressively than he had ever spoken before. Anger was welling up inside and he felt like throwing some nasty psionic blast into Max's pain receptors. He felt like forcing the street warrior to give Tzun more Slice. Foolish, Tzun cast the thought aside after considering what Max might do to him in return. Word on the streets was …

With the speed of thought, the diplomatic side of his personality surfaced and took over. "I'll be more careful," the boy promised. Max slowed, his unseen visage showing uncertainty, doubt. "Just give me a lesson and let me try again tomorrow," he coaxed. Then, after a painfully long pause, he added, "I can do this."

For the first time, Tzun thought he saw a flicker of doubt pass over Max's face. Confidence may have fled. He looked uncertain. But, retaining his ever present cover of coolness, Max looked over his shoulder and paused before saying anything: "Tomorrow kid. Take it easy tonight and meet me here tomorrow. We'll do a lesson after you get some rest." Then, in an uncharacteristic moment of charity, he spun half around and tossed Tzun a silver round worth more money than the boy had given Max a few moments before.

"Thanks!" Tzun responded in shock. *It worked!* Brushing Max's mind was probably a dangerous thing to do but Tzun hadn't really intended to do it at all. He just thought the thought and reaped the rewards. *I could make some serious money this way,* he considered, imagining a stream a wealthy women shopping on the far south side of Mariner's Market Street and emptying their purses as he massaged the sympathetic portions of their minds.

"Sure thing kid," Max answered as he turned around and began walking away from his newest client. Several moments later, as Max passed a second turn, he connected the dots and seriously considered skipping their next meeting.

4 片

On his way home from a wealthier part of town where beggars were typically unwelcomed, Tzun beamed with satisfaction. His pockets had grown so stuffed with money, he'd taken the time to lay several large bills flat on the inside of each of his shoes to hide his success. His hidden pocket was also brimming over with large bills and his regular pockets had grown too inconspicuous to pass for a beggar any longer. It was time to empty them and relax the rest of the evening. Still, he collected more monies as he walked home, though donations quickly grew smaller as he entered the poorer parts of town where he lived. Tzun was feeling particularly pleased with his newfound abilities when he spotted his cousin Koemi half walking, half jogging towards their common apartment. She was clearly distressed.

"Koemi!" he called, sporting a smile and a happier disposition than he'd known in years.

"Oh Tzun!" she answered with a clear look of relief on her face. "You're okay!"

That was the first Tzun had considered his family might have been seriously concerned about his failure to come home the night before. Truth be known, this wasn't his first night away from home but it was unusual enough that it passingly occurred to him that they might be worried. But then, he was so caught up in what he was doing that he hadn't considered it worth his time to report back home to assuage any fears they might have had.

"We were all scared for you after what happened in the park last night," she continued, now rushing towards him instead of towards the apartment. "Did you get hurt? What happened?"

"I'm fine. I just got tired and fell asleep," he exaggerated.

"But didn't you go to the park?" she pressed with unhidden confusion written all over her face.

"Yeah. Just like I said when I left last night. What happened?"

"How could you miss it?" she openly wondered, even more confused.

"Miss what?"

"The twister … the gang fight." Koemi stared at Tzun dumbfounded. "You didn't sleep at the park. You couldn't have missed it …"

"No. I slept at the park," Tzun answered. "Towards the south end though … I didn't see anything last night or this morning," he continued, a bit surprised and relieved at the same time. "I guess I was at just the right spot not to get involved." Then, after a pause, he added, "Koemi – we don't get twisters around here."

Koemi eyed him with suspicion and only passingly considered his correction. Tzun looked too well kempt to have been at the park. "Tzun, the whole park is a disaster. No one could have slept there. Some really strong winds passed through. Benches were upended, statues were knocked over, branches were scattered everywhere – even a tree was half uprooted. A dozen gang members were taken to the hospital and one kid was taken to the morgue. There is no way you could have missed all that. Where were you?"

It was clear Koemi thought he was lying – but he wasn't, not really. It took him a long time to respond, taking in the bad news – had he really been that close to so much trouble? "I didn't sleep on a bench Koemi – I slept on the ground next to some bushes and a tall tree." *That must be why I missed the gusts of wind*, he considered. He wondered how much more he could safely tell his cousin. "Everything was normal when I started to leave the park – apart from feeling pretty sick – so I just laid down on the ground to wait it out when I fell asleep." That was pretty much all true but Tzun felt a bit guilty over the blatant omissions. "I was towards the edge of the park so I guess I just missed the action – I'm sure glad I wasn't noticed," he added with sincere feelings of gratitude.

"Marie's really worried."

"She'll be okay in a few minutes," Tzun answered, putting his arm around his cousin's shoulders and softly pulling her towards their apartment. "I had a really good day today," he gushed, patting his notably padded pants pockets.

Koemi's eyes widened. "You lifted all that today?" she asked in disbelief.

"Nope. I decided to beg along the bay by Macys …"

"Nuh-uh. You know they don't let anyone beg down there. What have you really been up to?"

"I'm serious," Tzun answered defensively, recognizing that this story wasn't going to make much sense out of context so he'd have to stretch the truth a little again. "I had a little trouble like I expected but nothing too bad – just some dodging through back alleyways to outrun the cops …"

"Oh … you're a dummy. You're lucky we didn't have to bail you out of jail again."

Without considering Tzun's discovery of how to brush empathy receptors, she was entirely right. "It seems like things have been too tight lately," he explained. "I …"

"I think you better lie," Koemi interrupted. "Tell everyone you had some really good lifts again today or something but Kan's going to be really upset if he finds out you're risking another jail stint." Her eyes were warm. She was probably right and Tzun could see she was sincerely trying to help.

"Yeah," Tzun confessed. "But maybe I shouldn't say anything at all. Kan gets awfully upset when anyone admits they've been lifting."

Koemi rolled her eyes. It was true. Everyone in the home knew the bigger kids were all lifting but no one could say that in front of Kan without earning a severe tongue lashing. He was a businessman. Having the unadulterated appearance of honor and trustworthiness outside of the home meant everything to him. Even when honest business practices meant losing some profit, he did what he thought was right. And even though that didn't translate into a perfect home life, he couldn't face the truth that his own children lacked integrity or that his own inadequacy to provide for his family was partially to blame for their wayward paths.

"You're right," she conceded with a dismissive chuckle.

5 片

Tzun woke the next morning in the alleyway where he first met Max. Hidden behind the dumpster, he overheard Max meeting with the same aqua haired junkie he'd seen the day before. He couldn't see his face – or his hair – but he vividly recognized that frustrated voice.

Tzun could tell his equilibrium was off again today and he keenly felt those feelings of withdrawal, those horrible feelings of desperation for another dose of Slice. *How can I possibly continue this for two and a half more weeks?* he worried. Somehow, he needed to get larger doses. He reached into his pocket to make sure his extra vial of Slice was close at hand and then reached into his other pocket to determine how much money he was bringing for Max today. Two large bills were in his main pocket and another few large bills were in the hidden pocket. Although he couldn't remember much of what happened the night before, he vaguely remembered thinking that he needed to impress Max today.

Because of this distraction, Tzun barely noticed that both men were walking away, not just the aqua haired boy. Instantly springing to his feet, Tzun grabbed his head and pressed on his temples while stumbling around the dumpster. He could see that the sun was lower in the sky than it should be for his normal meeting time and felt confused over what was happening.

"Max!" he called, his voice revealing both a sense of

urgency and a good deal of confusion. The man in leather trappings stopped walking and turned around with his characteristic coolness to meet Tzun's gaze.

"Hey kid!" he called back. "Your looking sharp today. What gives? With new clothes, I'm guessing you have money to pay for Slice today instead of looking for handouts?"

Uncharacteristically, Tzun felt his dormant temper rising but also found himself distracted by looking at his new hoodie and T-shirt and wondering where they came from. As he looked over his new clothes, he noticed a Celtic ring wrapped around his left forefinger. It wasn't fancy but Tzun had never worn a ring before and it felt strange on his finger. He masked his surprise. And being accustomed to covering his emotions while looking for diplomatic solutions, Tzun extinguished his rising temper and looked to capitalize on their common interest.

"Yeah, I have more money today," he agreed. "You should be happy this morning." Tzun looked towards where the sun appeared to be hanging around the corner of the alleyway and wondered what time it was while reaching into his pocket to present his offering. Maybe Max had been planning to come back later?

The street warrior backtracked to where Tzun was standing and inspected the bills, pursing his lips in a frown and nodding his head. "Much better kid," he said while reaching into his pocket and pulling out a new vial of Slice. Stopping his hand midair, he looked at Tzun carefully and added: "are you sure you still want to go through with this? You look like Hades after Hercules beat him up and you've barely got enough energy to stand straight." He pulled the vial slightly closer to his body to encourage a serious response – or perhaps it was just his habitual tease.

Leaving one hand pressed against his temple while reaching for the vial with the other, Tzun answered with more confidence than Max would have expected: "Actually, I was wondering what it would take to get an extra dose," Tzun answered. "Do higher doses change anything? Would it enhance my abilities if I took more?"

That thought visibly startled Max.

"Don't worry," Tzun immediately reassured him. "I have more money. I worked late into the night to get some extra." He pulled another large bill out of his pocket.

Max greedily eyed the offering but covered it so quickly that Tzun saw nothing besides a blank look. What was he thinking? The street warrior reached inside his labyrinth of inside jacket pockets and pulled out another vial, swirled it, and watched the metallic brown swirls quickly settle.

"This stuff is unpredictable kid," Max started to explain. Tzun was starting to feel frustrated that Max never called him by name. "Extra doses help some people; extra doses do nothing for others. Sometimes it makes that craving worse you know? This is a dangerous game. Remember how I told you that? It's dangerous." Max's voice seemed off – like maybe he was uncertain if he was trying to convince Tzun not to take an extra dose or if he was trying to convince himself that he should refuse the money for his conscience's sake. Tzun crumpled his brow as he considered the possibilities. Maybe Max was just slipping on his junkie sales pitch.

"Right," Tzun agreed, reaching for the vial with a bill pressed between two of his fingers for an easy trade.

While Tzun hungrily downed the first vial, Max casually nodded, tipped his hat, and turned around, to walk away. "Kid's dangerous," he muttered to himself. "Nerdy half-pint Asian kid." Tzun heard nothing.

"Max," Tzun called from behind. "My lesson …"

The street warrior poorly feigned surprise as he turned around. "Oh, sorry kid. I almost forgot." Max stopped talking for a moment, stared intently into Tzun's eyes. "Alright Tzun, show me what you've been practicing."

Anyone who's taken lessons in anything would have known to expect that directive coming from an unprepared teacher but Tzun was completely taken off guard. Virtually every moment of his life on Slice had consisted of manipulating other people's minds – and he was pretty sure *that* wouldn't go over very well with a worn, street veteran. He hesitated too long.

"Come on kid, I haven't got all day. Let's see what you can do."

Feeling desperate, Tzun did the first thing that came into his mind: he made Max kiss the dumpster and waited to see how long it would take the man encased in leather to overcome the power of suggestion that Tzun threw at him.

It took longer than expected.

Although he was just as amused as any other kid his age would have been to watch a superior doing something absolutely ridiculous, Tzun also understood there were limits and he was starting to worry that Max would be getting pretty angry sometime soon and he couldn't let that happen. Concentrating carefully, Tzun focused his mind on brushing Max's mind in a way to generate empathy tinged with sadness. Then, as the kissing died off, Tzun tried something he hadn't tried before: he wiped those memories from Max's mind.

It worked.

"Come on kid, I haven't got all day. Let's see what you can do."

"I just did."

"Did what."

"Showed you what I've been practicing."

"What? I didn't see nothin' kid. Do it again."

"Okay," Tzun began to explain. Here is the deal. I've been working on influencing other people and I just wiped your memory of the last minute or so."

That didn't go over so well. "Don't feed me that bull," Max bellowed. "I'm not here to play games kid. Show me what you can do or the lesson is over." It was becoming abundantly clear that Max had a temper. Tzun made a note of that and pushed subtle feelings of calmness into Max's mind – but it wasn't enough.

"Alright," Tzun conceded. "Pull out your pad and pen." Annoyed, Max did as instructed. "Write down the time." Max scowled at Tzun and almost left again but Tzun was brushing his mind to be more patient and empathetic so he wouldn't leave. He wrote down the time. As soon as he did, Tzun did what he had been practicing. Without saying a word, he got Max to take off his jacket, knock out one hundred and fifty pushups, and then put his jacket back on, filter through the pockets, and give Tzun a couple extra vials of Slice – not enough to be noticed as missing but enough to serve as a healthy bonus for Tzun. He then wiped Max's memory of the last few activities while sending Max into shivers – feeling as if he was freezing on this bright Spring morning.

"Got it?" Tzun asked.

"Come on kid, I haven't got all day. Let's see what you can do." Max rubbed his arms quickly with his hands, trying to warm up.

"Pull out your pad and pen," Tzun instructed, brushing Max's mind for extra patience this time. Max did so without protest.

"What does it say?"

"8:43 a.m." After a notable pause, he added, "hey, that's my handwriting."

"What time is it now," Tzun pressed.

"Nearly 9:00."

"Do you feel cold?"

"Yeah kid, I'm cold. Let's get on with this." Tzun held out his hand towards Max with his hand closed and then spread it open as if releasing something into the air. Max began taking off his jacket.

"Did you just do that?" Max queried.

"Yeah. I made you do a bunch of pushups too but you don't remember do you?"

Max scowled in return.

"I'm not joshin' you," Tzun nearly laughed. "Try to do a few pushups." He massaged Max's mind to feel really interested in whatever might happen. Max only knocked out a few pushups before slowing considerably and then stopped after only doing a few more. Looking up at Tzun with a careful gaze, Max released a nervous chuckle.

"You're not kiddin'."

"Nope."

"Do you know what you could do with power like that kid?" Max squinted one eye, raised the opposing eyebrow. Both eyes glazed over as he seemed to turn over the possibilities. Tzun continued to brush his thoughts for empathy so he wouldn't be suspicious that Tzun may have already taken advantage of him. "You could make a lot of money. If you went gambling ..."

Philosophizing quickly came to an end as a cop rounded the corner and began interrogating the two about someone witnessing drug activity down this alleyway. While Max ran his smooth talk, Tzun wiped the officer's memory of anything related to the complaint, put the officer in seizures of fear until he began to cower behind the dumpster, motioned his hand as if tipping an invisible hat towards Max, and ran down the alleyway towards Mariner's Market Street.

6 片

Rain splattered over the Dark Uzzit, soaking his clothes so thoroughly that he considered his movement might be entirely impaired. He slithered across the rooftop with his eyes riveted on Max, the notorious drug lord who had been ruining this town. Ever since he'd arrived, more Uzzit incidents had been headlining the news. Preying mostly on young kids, the leather wrapped man wore his collar up, his fedora tilted backward, and his head low to protect himself from the rain.

To the Uzzit, it looked like the drug dealer was ashamed – and he should have been. He tracked him most of the evening and catalogued every stop: a fifteen year old girl by the corner of a small local gym; a twenty year old man (who looked like the kind of person any reasonable man would fear) met Max behind a condemned home; a fifteen or sixteen year old girl who looked a little rough for the wear begged for another chance and fell to her knees and then all fours as Max walked away without delivering any goods; a fourteen year old boy offered a few coins only to receive a sneer from Max before delivering some harsh words and a small vial in a vacant lot behind the old grocery store.

Jumping from roof to roof to track someone down might have been hard work for a normal man but Uzzit could do it quietly if they had some good practice under their belt. This was only an information gathering mission so he couldn't afford to be caught – every move had to be made with the utmost care. Revenge would come later.

7 片

Days passed and then an entire week and then a couple more days. Koemi had Tzun so concerned about the "Dark Uzzit" and the string of violent crimes that followed him that Tzun took extra precautions everywhere he went. Whenever he was begging or lifting, he made sure to avoid anyone with dark skin. Half Asian himself, he held few racist sentiments but wisdom dictated caution in situations like these. Even considering Tzun's growing powers and his knowledge of the area, he felt no match for an upcoming Uzzit thug. And although he estimated that he could probably buy himself enough time to make a clean getaway, he didn't know enough about this criminal to feel safe in that estimation so he continued to take precautions.

Besides, things were getting tougher at home. Apparently, the Dark Uzzit hit Kan's business the night before last. Kan wasn't sure he'd be able to make rent so Ba Tu and

Marie's family had to come up with extra to make up for the shortfall. That would have been fine except that Ba Tu couldn't work and Marie had to tend him twenty-four-seven. That left Tzun as the family's sole provider. And while he'd been able to control Kan's mind long enough to announce that he wouldn't require Tzun's family to pay extra rent, Kan reneged on the deal as soon as Tzun's influence wore thin. Tzun quickly realized that this game would ultimately prove nothing more than an energy drain but that didn't stop him from making Kan do things to embarrass himself in front of the family from time to time.

Increasing rent challenges aside, Tzun was making more money. But then again, the price of Slice daily grew steeper. Within the last two days, Tzun's entire stash of money had become history and he'd barely been able to afford a single vial of Slice the day before. Max claimed he needed a huge amount of cash to keep supplying Tzun because he "just didn't feel right about it." He worried that "Slice just wasn't good for Tzun." By now, the young boy guessed that Max was using this line on other kids too – it was nothing more than a sales gimmick.

Given the injustice, Tzun considered stealing an extra vial of Slice from Max every day – not enough to be noticed – and then wiping Max's memory clean. But the last time he tried brushing Max's mind, he felt Max resisting. Tzun concluded that Max was practicing defenses against psionic influences so lifting from him could prove unreasonably risky. Besides, every time Tzun obtained an extra vial of Slice, he downed it before the day was over. He didn't even have a full extra vial anymore – he drank half of that in a moment of desperation last week.

At this rate, lifting and begging using empathy brushings wasn't going to cut it. Tzun was going to have to step up his efforts to procure extra money or his family would be without a home and he'd have to start from scratch. Nearly two weeks had passed now. He couldn't risk starting over again – it was simply too costly. On the other hand, Tzun was getting used to having money available to him with less and less effort. Even yesterday, he'd briefly considered he might be able to make enough money without taking any drastic measures. But in the end, only optimism could posit such a course of action - people on the street only carried so much money.

Tzun also considered hitting Kan's competition. After all, Kan had reason to believe that they hired the hit on his business and now, Tzun was suffering from their actions. If he had to escalate his lifting efforts, it seemed that he ought to hit someone who deserved it. Then again, he wasn't a burglar, never would be. On the other hand, he could always wipe clean any witness' memory if it was a one time knock off.

After habitually checking his pockets, Tzun unfolded a piece of paper in his pocket he didn't remember putting there. That was one thing about Slice that was still unnerving. Blackouts were not uncommon. In fact, it seemed to Tzun that he had them nightly. He scarcely remembered what happened past dinner time on any given night of the week. Half the time, he didn't even return home – and that was generating daily tongue lashings from his otherwise gentle mother who knew something wasn't right. At least, her lectures focused on encouraging Tzun to stay far away from the Dark Uzzit who seemed to be terrorizing the entire west bank of Puget Sound. And Marie was easy to control: the slightest mind brushing sent her into a state of calmness that made Tzun jealous – what would it be like to have such peace of mind like that? He'd forgotten.

The paper spelled out the address of Kan's competition, the time doors locked, the location of the alarm system, and the time police patrolled the area the night before. *At least I know where I was last night,* Tzun nervously joked to himself. He went to the bathroom to check his stash of cash. Although he distinctly remembered running out of cash the day before, he was growing accustomed to finding surprises in his secret places. Since he didn't remember anything he'd done the night before, it stood to reason that he would likely have done something to alleviate that problem. Besides, there wasn't anything in the secret fold of his pants and the cash in his pocket would barely be enough to keep Max happy.

But there was nothing there. *Blasted bricks!* he all but screamed to himself. He was pretty sure that Max would sell him one vial of Slice for the money in his pocket but there wouldn't be enough for the two he was getting accustomed to and certainly there wasn't enough for three. He swore again, this time out loud, and pounded his fist on the counter.

"You alright?" his mother called.

"Fine," he brashly answered. Marie hesitated for a moment and then walked away, her face transparent with concern. Since birth, Tzun had rarely showed any signs of a temper so these recent outbursts left her terribly unnerved. Something was intolerably wrong.

Then, Tzun had an idea that hadn't occurred to him before: even though Tzun could appreciate the aqua haired man's frustrations with Max, it was pretty clear he was a bad egg – perhaps as bad as they get. The city would be better off without someone like him having strong Uzzit powers at their fingertips. If Tzun hurried now, he could arrange a Slice lift from the aqua haired man before his meeting with Max. The timing would be difficult but he thought he could pull it off if he was careful. So, he rushed out the door, ran down to the docks and situated himself opposite the side of the alleyway where the aqua haired man habitually left his meetings with Max. Passingly, Tzun wondered how he could meet Max every day at the same place, yell loudly enough to attract attention from either end of the alleyway, and never get bothered by the police for a drug bust. He wondered if this guy was buying them out to leave him alone.

After doling out so much money to Max, Tzun was beginning to understand this new culture enjoyed by the aqua haired junkie. At times, he had money to spare, money to buy new clothes, money to eat at sit down restaurants, and if he'd wanted to, money to buy out a cop or two. That freedom was swiftly dissipating as Slice prices were rising but Tzun had been starting to enjoy that lifestyle … even if it only lasted half a week. Perhaps, Tzun considered, he was even beginning to expect that lifestyle. And he was beginning to understand that he couldn't want to go back to how things were; he couldn't live a life where he was daily scrounging around for a few dollars, where he was a slave to the daily grind.

Tzun arrived earlier than expected and patiently listened as the usual tone of exchange passed between the parties: the aqua man grumbled, swore, and complained; Max brushed him off without the slightest care for whatever he had to say. This time however, Max threw a surprise wrench into the system. In a voice that Tzun could barely hear at all, he warned the aqua haired man. "Listen. I hear you. I have problems too but here's the deal: the last supply of Slice has to be double whatever you've been using. If you don't bring double the money, you don't get the Slice. If you don't get the Slice, you start from day one. Got it? In two days, you need to bring double the money or you're back to square one. I can't fix all of your troubles. All I can do is deliver the goods, right?" Then, tipping his hat, Max turned around to find a spot on the sofa, pulled his fedora over his eyes, and reclined as if he was going to take a nap before his next client arrived.

The man with aqua hair stormed off, swearing a stream of profanities as usual, and flew out the alleyway exactly the way Tzun expected he would. Throwing a strong psionic blast of loathing, hatred, and anger towards the aqua haired man, Tzun directed all of the negative feelings towards the newest vial of Slice in the man's possession. Further brushing his mind, Tzun made the man pull the vial of Slice out of his pocket and throw it as hard as he could into Puget Sound, quickly turning his head away from the vial and swearing a new string of expletives. While his head was turned, Tzun psionically pulled the vial towards himself at breakneck speed, caught the vial of Slice, slid it into his secret pocket, and rounded the corner into the alleyway. Behind him, he heard a loud splash as the aqua man's senses returned and he realized what he'd done. Even if the vial had landed in the water, the search would have been futile. But, *that's what junkies do,* Tzun thought remorsefully. He knew that feeling of desperation too well. He almost felt sorry for him.

"Hey kid, how are you doin' today?" Max gushed before pulling the fedora away from his eyes. Tzun guessed his footsteps were familiar, easily recognized.

"I'm okay," Tzun answered, characteristically using as few words as possible and holding out the money to trade for a new vial of Slice. Max barely looked at it and made the trade without further comment.

"You look great kid," Max answered. "You workin' out? You look like you're gainin' weight."

The comment surprised Tzun. He certainly wasn't working out but he did notice that his muscles were often sore when he woke up in the mornings. What was he doing in the evenings? Now that he thought about it, he ran all the way to the docks this morning without running out of breath – that was new. "I don't know," Tzun answered, trying to brush aside the comment.

"You don't know?"

"Nope."

"You still blackin' out?" Max asked as if he was deeply concerned – but the artificial tone of voice offended Tzun. Apart from his mother and Koemi, there wasn't anyone in the world that genuinely cared about Tzun and he was used to that. He didn't like people pretending to step into those shoes, especially drug peddlers.

"Maybe," he answered evasively.

"Tzun," Max said. That surprised the young boy. Max never spoke his name. "Look at me." Tzun no longer noticed it but he rarely made eye contact with anyone. Beggars and thieves are careful not to look into people's eyes. That's just what they do. Awkwardly, Tzun looked up into Max's piercing eyes. "Dude. Slice doesn't usually keep people blacking out for two weeks, you know? A few days, yeah. A week … *maybe*. Two weeks?"

"It hasn't been two weeks," Tzun corrected.

"Yeah but we're like a day or two away right?"

"Two."

"Well then, same thing," Max said, leaking a tone of aggression. "It's not good. Two weeks is way too long. That's bad news kid." But then, after a pause, he changed course a little, "but you're looking healthier. You been gettin' hurt during your blackouts?"

"Sometimes."

"Bad?"

Tzun hated getting grilled like this. He just wanted to down his daily dose of Slice and to get out of there. Max's lessons were worthless and Tzun was starting to learn things that Max could do – like tearing things. He hadn't tried anything like the dumpster yet but he thought he might be able to do it. He wanted to try. "Not really," he answered evasively again.

"How bad?"

"What does it matter Max?" Tzun answered in frustration. "I'm walking; I'm breathing; I'm okay." Before Max could respond, Tzun's temper flaired. He downed the Slice while Max rambled on about something Tzun wouldn't hear and then turned. Making a forceful upward movement with one hand and a violent downward swing with the other, Tzun looked like someone throwing a ball into the air and then swatting it back down, only his hands were frozen in clawing shapes. The dumpster flew into the air a good four feet before smashing back down onto the ground, producing a horrendous tearing sound as it landed. Chips of asphalt flew towards the two men but Tzun deflected them without thinking about them at all. Tzun noted four tears zigzagging their way down the entire length of the dumpster and looked over at Max with proud satisfaction. He didn't feel angry any more. He felt excited. He loved the way Slice made him feel. He wanted to do it again – and Max always made him do his tricks twice so he expected he would.

But Max didn't return the look. The veteran drug lord looked at the dumpster with shock and something else. Was that fear? "Ain't nobody doin' that," he jabbered softly. "Holy bloody bricks," he breathily whispered. "Kid, that's …"

"I've been practicing," Tzun interrupted, pleased that he'd finally impressed his mentor. Now, maybe he could get some good lessons.

"Wwhhoooow … You've got serious swag kid," Max answered, diplomatically starting to walk away with a big, fake smile spreading over his face. "Yup, that's seriously impressive. Keep practicing that and by next week, you'll be demolishing entire buildings!" he called over his shoulder as he adopted his characteristic cool strut down the alleyway.

The compliment wasn't well received. Tzun wanted another bottle of Slice and now, with all hopes of any decent lessons shot, he was feeling angry again. Without thinking about what he was doing, he reached his hand out towards Max who was now a good fifteen feet away and made a pulling motion with his hand as if plucking a stubborn apple off a low hanging branch. Max's arms spread wide open as if someone had grabbed both of his sleeves to pull off his jacket. Then, Tzun spun and yanked his hand backwards and slightly over his shoulder as if throwing a fast pitch. Max's jacket violently flew towards his hand. Behind Tzun, he heard a shoulder pop as it tore out of joint; the street warrior's agonizing yelp following almost immediately. Tzun threw a major psionic blast towards Max to further incapacitate him. Fear receptors and pain receptors flew towards overload and while Tzun began collecting vials of Slice from Max's jacket, he raised his hand towards Max and then threw the drug lord across the alleyway and onto the junky couch leaning against the wall. While Max cowered into the corner of the couch, moaning in pain, Tzun casually walked towards him, dumped the dozen or more vials of Slice into his pockets, and then tossed the jacket onto the couch next to Max. When Tzun hit the end of the alleyway, he wiped Max's memory clean so that the last thing he remembered was sitting on the couch and arguing with the aqua haired man over how many doses of Slice were required to complete the two week cycle.

8 片

Tzun sat alone near the edge of the park, shaking in disbelief. He couldn't believe what he'd just done. Never in his life had he seriously hurt anyone. He'd barely entertained any thoughts of seriously hurting anyone. It just wasn't in his nature. He didn't even know how - until now.

There he was, huddling in a corner after single handedly taking out the legendary drug lord and the only dealer of Slice anyone knew about. Tzun needed nineteen vials of Slice before it would stay permanently in his system – that was counting his second dose for today and a double dose for the last day. He downed his second dose for the day and counted thirteen vials in his pocket. *Six shy*, he realized in horror. What were the chances he could get any more vials from Max? Even with his memory wiped – or perhaps because his memory had been swiped – he would surely guess that Tzun had stolen the missing Slice vials. Maybe he could only drink one dose a day … No, that might reduce his powers. If anything, he needed extra doses for the last few days …

Passingly, Tzun realized how quickly his thoughts had gone from feeling badly over what he had done to feeling badly that he didn't have enough Slice to make it through his three weeks. He felt ashamed. Then, old habits sunk deep into his psyche and he began recycling rationales to justify his actions: Max preyed on kids; he charged too much; he lied; he didn't deliver the lessons he promised; and now he was pushing Tzun to plan burglaries just to make ends meet. No, Max didn't deserve pity.

Where's Koemi, he wondered. She frequently came to the park this time of the morning. Why wasn't she here? He needed someone to talk to and she was the only one he could trust to help him out without giving him a lecture. He waited for an hour and then another. He waited until he lost his patience and then, as his temper flared, he dashed out of the park like a man fixin' to do something bad. Tzun recognized this unfamiliar feeling and checked it, if only for a little while.

Besides, he had to be careful tonight. The Dark Uzzit had been headlining again. Deaths were mounting. Almost all of them were gang related. Tzun took some consolation from that fact but still ... he had enough challenges. He didn't need any confrontation with the Uzzit thug.

9 片

Lightening flashed, thunder roared, and rain splattered over the concrete, bricks, and mortar, making a sound like splashing grease in a deep fryer. The dark Uzzit clung to his clothes and wrapped them tightly around himself. Why did he always have to have such bad weather while following the infamous drug lord? *At least it makes it easier to stay under cover,* he consoled himself. He leaped from one rooftop to the next, padding his landings by slightly levitating himself so that he could retain a cloak of silence. The feeling was addicting. He practically felt like he was flying.

Peaking over the ledge to observe the activity below, he watched as Max met his usual customers. The dark Uzzit carefully noted the dispositions of each client and watched as Max passed on vials of Slice to each of them. When he met the man behind the condemned home, the dark Uzzit couldn't bear to watch. That man shouldn't have Slice. He was a danger to society already. With Slice, the man would be a danger to everyone around him. Someone had to take him out. When Max left, the dark Uzzit dove off the building as the twenty-something man rounded the corner on the other edge of the street. Landing mere inches in front of the man, the dark Uzzit glared into the eyes of the budding criminal.

"You have something of mine," he declared.

"Like h ..."

Before the man could finish his retort, the dark Uzzit sent the man flying through the air and smashing into the brick wall behind him. When he failed to fall unconscious, the dark Uzzit sent him through the air and into another brick wall on the opposing side of the street. *I hope that didn't break the vial of Slice,* he instinctively worried. Moments later, he was downing the vial and jumping onto the nearest rooftop to watch over the drug lord a little longer.

10 片

Tzun woke up behind the dumpster. *Blasted Bricks!* he swore to himself. The last thing he needed was another encounter with Max – especially since he wouldn't enjoy the element of surprise a second time. Confident that Max wouldn't be accepting any belated apologies, Tzun had stayed away from this alleyway since he lifted Slice from Max several days past. Quietly and instinctively, he reached into his pocket. It was there. His last vial of Slice. He was still five shy. He wasn't sure where he got the extra vial but he vaguely remembered thinking the night before that he would have to steal Slice from other Uzzit. Maybe that was why he was here. *But Max always leaves the same way as the aqua haired man,* he reconsidered. Then, rethinking the issue, he remembered that they never left together either. *What will happen now that Max isn't meeting with me?*

He didn't know. As he considered standing up to hide somewhere down the docks where the aqua haired man would be passing by, he heard footsteps rounding the corner. *That's Max.* The footsteps were unmistakable.

Tzun retreated a little further behind the dumpster, its

misshapen form resembling some avant garde sculpture. Max's footsteps came closer and then briefly hesitated before plopping down onto the couch not five feet away from Tzun. With little more than a few empty cardboard boxes keeping Tzun out of Max's sight, the young boy grew nervous. When a second set of footsteps rounded the corner and the daily banter between the drug lord and the junkie began, Tzun downed his last vial of Slice. No reserves, no resources, and no viable hope for getting his last day and a half's worth of Slice, Tzun would have felt discouraged and depressed but for that electric buzz that trickled down his throat and into his stomach. It was taking longer for him to feel energized but the effects were still noticeable.

If Tzun attacked Max after the aqua haired man left, before Max saw him, and before he had a chance to react … Tzun felt torn. Part of him felt sorry for Max, sorry for what he had done. Part of him felt desperate. But he couldn't go back to the life he'd had before. After tomorrow, he could get his own apartment. Maybe he could get a job. Even though he looked scrawny, he could prove his new strength easily enough. Maybe he could work loading ships at the dock. If he brushed a few minds with empathy, he might even be able to get a job that paid well …

"Hey kid, you're looking sharp today," Max greeted the aqua haired man. Tzun couldn't see the young man but he could hear an exasperated breath escape clenched teeth. At twenty one years old, he didn't like being called a child. Small talk continued only briefly. No lesson ensued. Max exited the alleyway towards Mariner's Market Street while the aqua haired man wearily walked the opposing direction. Tzun disagreed with Max: he looked like Hades frozen over. Tzun wasn't swift with mythology but he recognized a ragged man when he saw one.

He stepped out from behind the dumpster.

"Hey kid," he called. The aqua haired man turned around, instant anger in his countenance.

"What do you want," he snapped back, pulling a long

bowie knife out of a side holster and rushing towards Tzun before bothering to hear any response. Tzun was caught by surprise. A moment earlier, his quickly improvised plan had been to simply brush the young man's mind again and then wipe it clean while he was leaving. This wasn't quite how he planned things.

The aqua haired man lunged at Tzun who had no time to play intricate psionic games. Instinct took over. Tzun leaped backwards while waving his arm towards his attacker as if shoving clothes on a hanger sideways. The dumpster flew sideways and pinned the aqua haired junkie against the wall, blood splattering in every direction around the dumpster. Without thinking, Tzun threw the dumpster back to the side of the alleyway where it belonged and pulled the Slice vial out of his front pocket where the aqua haired man always stashed it. The vial was cracked and broke open as Tzun pulled it out, forcing him to instantly down the Slice and clean up every slight spill that came out of the vial. As the electric buzz glistened down his throat, Tzun felt a scratching feeling as well – a small piece of glass passed down his windpipe.

As the adrenaline rush passed and as Tzun finished drinking the Slice, he looked over the bloody corpse of the young man Tzun had never spoken to – before today. Disgust and revulsion overwhelmed him as he considered what he had done. He nearly wretched at the thought of what had just happened but he forced the Slice to stay down. *Only four left,* he intuitively reminded himself. *Only four left.* He felt ashamed, scared, perhaps angry. But he needed to press on.

11 片

The Dark Uzzit leaped from rooftop to rooftop, following the same pattern he had followed before. Max was increasingly predictable. As he peered over the edge of the grocery store, the Dark Uzzit watched as the fourteen year old boy pulled out a stash of money much larger than he had the night before. Max smiled, delivered the vial, and sent the boy away happy as a lamb.

The Dark Uzzit hated Max for what he did. Ruining children; ruining families; ruining society; the man represented everything foul. But tonight was the time to clean up the city. He just needed to wait: two more drops.

Only a slight sprinkle of rain dripped out of the sky, leaving the Dark Uzzit feeling somewhat grateful for the reprieve. He needed a break from the bad weather – it was depressing. Max slithered down the streets, pushing his last two deals with a degree of nonchalance that one only achieves after many years of experience. The last drop was to a girl that couldn't have been any older than twelve. The Dark Uzzit fumed. There was no excuse for preying on children that small. Thin of frame, long of hair, and as cute as any girl the Dark Uzzit had ever seen, the young girl was nearly giddy about the small vial of Slice she held in her hands. *She is only three or four days into this*, he reminded himself, keeping tabs of every drop.

Max hurriedly rounded the corner. *Here we go!* the Dark Uzzit gloated, carefully holding his leather hood over his head to obscure his face as he jumped from rooftop to rooftop. Black sludge smeared across his face, the Dark Uzzit nearly looked like a guerilla fighter smacking down a rival drug lord's territory. Tonight he sported new shoes, thick black jeans, leather boots, and leather jacket that kept him warmer than usual – or perhaps he just felt warm because of the weather.

Two guards stopped Max as he made his way to the entrance. These were new guards. As Max gave them the proper password, they let him pass by. *Now!* The instant Max passed behind closed doors, the Dark Uzzit dove face first off of the roof of a four story building and all but flew down to the guards. Twisting his body, levitating his own weight, and throwing knives at the two guards, he landed softly. Aimed well, there was little needed to finish the job. He really had no clue where he was going. He only knew that this was where Max got Slice. This was production headquarters.

He tried to be quiet but his new shoes plodded on the hardwood floor louder than he could control. Pretty soon, he turned a corner only to catch the attention of a half dozen men who perfunctorily pulled out their guns and began shooting. Instinct took over. Years of discouragement, frustration, untamed fears, and anger flooded his mind. Untold horrors returned to haunt the Dark Uzzit as he looked upon these men as vultures preying on young kids. With a wave of his hand, a wave of bullets wafted off to his side, missing their target and ringing loudly as they ricocheted off of metal filing cabinets. He sent out a universal and massive psionic blast to puncture the pain receptors of everyone present. Everyone except Max fell to the ground holding their ears and screaming in pain as blood trickled out of their noses. One knocked over a tray of Slice vials as he fell to the ground. Instinctively, the Dark Uzzit summoned a number of vials to his hand and shoved them into his pocket, saving one and popping the cork so that he could down the contents and cast the vial off to the side.

Max looked over at this strange intruder while trying to maintain a psionic barrier protecting him from the attacks of this stranger. He was only barely succeeding and knew it wouldn't last. He'd heard about this Dark Uzzit. Apart from the sludge on his face, he didn't look as intimidating as he expected. About five foot nine, medium build, and dressed in black, the dark Uzzit looked too undersized to deserve the reputation he had been accumulating over the past weeks.

"Game's over Max," the Dark Uzzit declared in the most ominous voice he could muster. The voice was familiar and far from intimidating but Max couldn't place it.

"Hey kid, what do you want?" Max asked with his characteristic charisma but the dark Uzzit knew the questions were only to stall time: backups would be coming. "You need more Slice? We have plenty here…"

"I have enough. I want you to stop dealing to little

kids. Twelve is a bit young don't you think?"

Max thought he identified the voice now but he wasn't sure. "Tzun? It's you right? That talented kid who …"

"Stop dealing to little kids. Got it? I know your route; I know every drop; you gotta stop or …"

Two new guards inconspicuously burst into the room and started popping off shots at the dark Uzzit. Untamed, his anger surged until he found himself raging out of control. Bullets wafted aside once more, the Dark Uzzit sent such strong psionic blasts that every guard in the room fell over dead. Max screamed out in pain but remained standing – barely. Four more guards entered the room and then five. Each fell in turn, recoiling in horrendous fear until they ran out of the room shooting at whoever was coming towards them. Four guards in the hallway fell from this new rampage.

Thankful for the temporary distraction, Max diverted his energies to psionically throw metal filing cabinets at the intruder. Flanking the intruder on both sides, the cabinets threatened to sandwich the Dark Uzzit and kill him quickly.

But it didn't work.

The Dark Uzzit diverted the cabinets, smashing them into the ground and twisting them into a knotted, unrecognizable mess. Then, his subconscious urged him to do something he hadn't done before. Frustrations, insecurities, and anger that had remained deeply hidden his entire life suddenly found their exit and their expression: the cabinets imploded until they burst into flames, dripping liquid metal all over the ground as they shot towards Max. One horrific scream later and the warehouse fell silent apart from the sound of flames lapping at tables near the fallen drug lord.

The Dark Uzzit willed the flames to die and they did. He pulled several more vials of Slice towards himself and downed a third of them. The rest, he would drink tomorrow and that would be it. The three weeks would be over.

12 片

Tzun woke up in his own bed. He couldn't remember the last time he actually woke up in his own bed. How long had it been? One week? Three? He reached over to pull the blankets down and saw blood all over the sheets and his hands. Scared, he quickly sat up and looked around. Traces of blood decorated his pillows and the floor. Half terrified, half shocked, Tzun darted into the bathroom to clean himself off. If his family saw him like this … Kan would surely kick his entire family out of the house. But then, maybe that didn't matter anymore. Today was the last day. He reached into his pocket – a new pocket in new pants – and found eight vials of Slice. *Why the extra?* he wondered.

No matter. He drank four in quick succession, saving the rest for his last afternoon dose. Not remembering the night before, he couldn't recall ever drinking four vials of Slice in one day. What would he be able to do with that much Slice in his system?

As he looked in the mirror, he saw the rest of his new clothes all splattered in blood - but not as badly as he expected. Dried blood came off of the leather jacket easily enough and the blood on his pants and boots was relatively hard to see. He scrubbed them well and hoped they would dry quickly. With no washer or dryer in the house and with no change of clothes, Tzun was accustomed to wearing wet clothes when he washed them. It was inconvenient but he didn't care much – besides, he would soon be living in a place with nice appliances wouldn't he? If anything, it made it fun to wear wet clothes one last time.

Tzun showered, wrapped himself in a clean towel, and darted back to his room, hoping not to be seen and then gathered his blood soaked bedding into a pile where he could clean them later – or maybe he would just throw them away.

He was going to have plenty of money now. Satisfied that his new clothes did not conspicuously show significant amounts of blood, he put them back on and resisted the urge to jump out the window onto the ground below. He felt such an amazing burst of energy that he was barely able to contain himself. Four vials of Slice was too much, he quickly decided, feeling like a ten year old boy who had been cooped up in a car for ten hours of travelling - desperately awaiting the moment when he could open the door and run as long as his legs would allow. Energy swirled inside Tzun's body, insisting he do something to release it.

Convinced he'd escaped anyone's attention this morning and feeling happier than he had ever felt in his entire life, Tzun bounced around the corner from his room into the family room where his disposition dramatically changed.

Kan lay dead on the floor, his hands tightly gripping a shotgun and his face grotesquely twisted, frozen in anger. A spray of shotgun bullets traced along his face and more particularly, across his eyes. Ba Tu lay dead by his side, a crazy smile spread across his face as if he had been watching something amusing – he always looked like that. Dried blood coagulated in a stream where it had come out of his ears, mouth, and nose.

Cousins, huddled on the other side of the room with their mothers also lay dead. Tzun's own mother and Koemi lay crumpled in front of them as if they had been kneeling, perhaps pleading for help. Red liquid splattered all around them gave the appearance that something – or someone – had exploded. Tzun recoiled in horror as he beheld the scene and started putting the pieces of the puzzle together. He looked more carefully around the room. Bloody footsteps traced back into his room where they led to his bed. The front door was ajar. A policeman's glock lay on the ground next to the door.

Memories started flooding back: Kan's verbal attack; his mother's pleading; his aunt's chastisement; Kan's shooting; Tzun's uncontrollable anger; his blackout; the officer's arrival and subsequent memory wipe; Tzun's feeling of confusion as he saw everyone dead; and then, another blackout.

Tzun reeled in confusion again. At that moment, Tzun's split psyche underwent the Slice transformation that usually came much quicker and much easier. With this last dose, Tzun gained the ability to choose. He could leave the room as an awkward, passive, gentle teenage boy or he could leave as the Dark Uzzit. Tzun fell to his knees in anguish as he saw two paths lying before him. He preferred his true self, the resourceful teenage boy trying to take care of his family, but there was nothing left for him there. Only poverty, insecurity, fear of abuse, thievery, and an ever growing number of painful memories remained. There was nothing more. He couldn't live that life. He couldn't choose that.

Wiping his own memories clean, he downed four more vials of Slice and jumped out the window. Leaping from rooftop to rooftop, he wound his way through the docks and the city until he arrived at the warehouse.

As he entered the main room, he found a single man sitting at a desk, holding his hand as if he had just hung up a phone, shaking his head in disbelief. Everything about him from his dress to his demeanor screamed that he was in charge of the entire operation. The instant he saw Tzun, he recoiled somewhat in surprise.

"Who are you?" he asked gruffly.

"I'm Max's replacement."

"Would that make you the Dark Uzzit?" he queried with a clear dose of doubt in his voice. "You're not so dark."

"Want proof?" Tzun groused in response. Metal cabinets, tables, chairs, and dozens of other items began to rumble. Glass equipment fell from countertops and shattered. Building walls shook ominously. But before Tzun ventured to do anything further, the man sat back in his chair and dismissively waived his hand at Tzun, pulling a cigarette out of its box.

"That's alright," he answered casually as he snapped open a metal lighter and lit the stick in his mouth. "You got this figured out right? It's never permanent. You'll always need another dose to keep your power. Only I know how to make Slice so I'm still in charge. Got it?"

"Got it."

"Sit down. Let's go over the numbers."

They haggled.

BORING STUFF ABOUT DREW

After graduating from BYU (Phi Kappa Phi) with degrees in history, music, and logic, Drew entered the J. Reuben Clark Law School on scholarship and began teaching philosophy at UVU.

LESS BORING STUFF ABOUT DREW

Forsaking exotic and life-changing trips around the world with jazz bands (Europe) and symphonies (China and the Philippines) and recording on CDs (only three), Drew focused his attention upon a much more useful talent: helping people beat each other up with reams of paperwork that cost ridiculous amounts of money. As a part of sacred legal tradition, those expensive novellas are only read by an embarrassingly small group of people who are required by ancient statute to believe they are better than you.

Drew won his very first case straight out of law school: a $25,000,000,000 (yes, you read that correctly: 25 billion dollars) international tort case that was appealed to the United States Supreme Court. Carefully dodging any potential backlash of fame and fortune, his legal career was depressingly less glamorous so he returned to his true love: storytelling.

SORT OF COOL STUFF ABOUT DREW

While in law school, Drew thrust his obsessive compulsive personality disorder into a good cause: he returned to his childhood juggling addiction. Drew was awarded Utah's Best Professional Juggler award in 2001 and has retained that title ever since (mostly because they quit having the competition but he likes to brag about it anyway). He juggled as a performer at the 2002 Salt Lake Olympics and competed at the 2006 International Juggler's Association. He handily lost because he dropped too much, but at least he saved one drop with an epic sidekick that audibly wowed the judges! Drew was a staple performer at the Timpanogos Storytelling Festival for more than a dozen years because he is the only juggler in the world that tells stories while juggling. Really. He bills himself as the Story Juggler.

SIGN UP FOR DREW'S NEWSLETTER AT http:// anewbreedofdragon.com

You'll get a free short story from bestselling author David Farland and a free short story from Drew Briney. You'll also receive occasional updates on new books, stories, and events. No spam. No email sharing.

Opening the Grave
Some Things are Better Left Undone

SHADOW COULDN'T STOP MOVING. Enslaved by his feet, he plodded along like some halfhearted marionette who wanted nothing more than to cut the strings controlling his body. He didn't mind hiking and he didn't mind following the earth's promptings, but this particular trek seemed excessive. Two days had passed. With very little food and almost no rest, Shadow had hiked past the outer ridges of town, through the sparse edges of Eznaki Forest, straight across the sandy dunes of Azh'leniki, and deep into the eerie interior of Vanaleige Forest.

His blistered feet smoldered but he refused to look at them. Somehow, it seemed seeing them might make the burning worse. Besides, more intense discomforts vied for his attention. Occasional coughs were slight but they ignited his lungs with fiery sensations he couldn't begin to describe. He'd practically drowned himself earlier that morning. Thirsty as sun-bleached lips on a wooden totem, Shadow had been careless when he came across the only waterway remotely close to Azh'leniki: he'd fallen in head first. It hurts to breathe in nearly as much water as you drink. He could have guessed that before - but now he knew. Now every full breath was a reminder and every cough was an unwelcome castigation for his foolishness.

Although these physical challenges were far from negligible, a visceral foreboding began to overshadow their presence, threatened to consume his soul with a suffocating, dreadful haunting. Shadow slowed his step, considered possibilities. Perhaps this was the earth preparing him for his own death. As azh'nahn, he deserved it. He accepted that truth even though deep down, he didn't truly comprehend it. No matter what the earth asked of him, it was his duty to obey. That truth he accepted without reservation. Nevertheless, as ethereal hauntings continued, Shadow grew increasingly convinced that he didn't *want* to do whatever she was asking of him right now.

Already, he was considering his trip home. This time, he wouldn't be in such a rush and he would pamper his feet. This time, his pace would be reasonable. He'd probably take extra time to walk around the burning dunes instead of plowing a straight path through every foreseeable obstacle. He'd rest in the shade and stay close to rivers.

And he'd sleep.

Without intending to, Shadow stopped walking, paused to uncork his nearly empty flagon of water, and sucked hard to get the last drizzles of water before falling to his knees. When he replaced the cork, he crumbled to all fours, contemplated what might be next. The jagged cut of his pants left one knee uncovered as he began to crawl and his knuckles quickly turned white from holding his bo staff too tightly as he dragged it along the ground. Shadow paused, trembled a little as the foreboding grew and a startled bird fluttered out of a nearby bush. *This is crazy*, he thought. But he was too intimidated to say it out loud. Shivering and consumed by a harrowing fear of whatever lay ahead, Shadow actually felt more comfortable crawling than walking.

Not far ahead, a ledge taunted him, dared him to visit, to peer over the valley below. Maybe this was the end of the journey. Maybe the ledge would betray him. Perhaps it was a stone elemental. Perhaps it would toss him to his death. As he crawled into its inviting lap, Shadow froze, felt his bare stomach next to the cool earth, and obeyed her call to stay put. The smell of putrid soil wafted past his nostrils. Involuntarily, he nearly heaved, shifted to breathing through his mouth to minimize the smell of rotting … something. He pushed his long hair to the side, let his finger linger on a scar along his neck, shamefully considered the embarrassing failure it represented.

Shadow lay motionless for many long moments, staring at the oddly familiar valley. It seemed he'd been here before but he couldn't be sure. If he had been here, he'd visited the valley from some other vantage point, perhaps from the hills on the other side. Still, the area exuded such a haunting feeling that he couldn't imagine forgetting the slightest detail. Every contorted tree branch seemed a tale of torture, the history of some foul deed. No flowers bloomed, though the season was late enough to demand their presence. Even the grasses seemed yellowish, sickly from some disease. Shadow observed that they matched the demented, spiraling lichen trails that hung from tree branches like loosely braided beards.

A nest of fire ants drew threateningly close. Their large size left Shadow more than mildly uncomfortable. He remembered hearing of a distant cousin who'd died from their stings but despite the memory, his resolve stiffened and he refused to move. He was here for a reason. Until that reason was fulfilled, he would lie motionless as the frozen peaks of Ishmandool. Still, he shuddered when he tried to discern the foreboding.

He'd been raised to trust the earth's promptings, to have

confidence in his instincts. Years of training had given him the discipline to push through his fear, to trust the earth but that didn't put an end to his curiosity, his attempt to make some sense out of what was happening. He considered several options but none of them felt right, so he landed on the only idea that made any sense whatsoever. Mother Earth was testing him. That was it: a test. He didn't know why she would do that but there was no other explanation to be found. Why else would she send azh'nahn to observe whatever doom he was about to witness? He had no power to change anything and no position to influence how the Hiwalani might deal with whatever he might see. He was practically Trayki. But despite his lowly status, he held fast to his determination. If the earth wanted him to observe something, he would watch carefully.

A brief gust of mist-ridden wind distracted Shadow's thoughts and blew his long hair over his eyes. He shook his head, tossing the hair to one side, shifted his eyes to the right and then left. Apart from the fire ant nest, there was no sign of moving life. While he found the thought slightly disturbing, it made sense. No healthy animal would graze in such sallow grass. And if there were no grazing animals, there would be no large predators. He saw no birds. He'd probably heard the only bird brave enough to land here a few moments past. This infested land was barely worthy of insect life, let alone the lives of larger, more sacred beasts. Perhaps, Shadow considered, some cursed creatures fed on insects or the black, putrid fungi that threatened to overtake some of the larger trees but none were to be seen. The foreboding pointed to something else.

Just as Shadow seriously considered he'd made a mistake and needed to move to a different vantage point, he heard shouting below. Amber hair and bronze skin immediately identified two men as Hiwalani. Shadow was numbered among this race of mages but these men did not share his lowly status. These were Hinzwala, men and women whose job it was to explore the limits of magical forms, Hiwalani elite who lived off donations from the Hiwalani masses. Their skin was a lighter shade of bronze because they spent much of their time studying indoors.

Shadow recalled his mother teaching him how it was unnatural for people to spend so little time tilling the earth, working the ground, and expressing themselves through the arts. But Shadow considered that maybe higher Hinzwalan magic forms were expressions of art. Maybe Hinzwalan forms connected mages more deeply with the earth than Hiwalani magic. Then again, maybe his mother was right. These men had very little free time. How could anyone connect with the earth when they had so little time to rest, to become one with themselves?

A woman joined the two men below. She was old. Even from this distance, Shadow could easily discern her prominent crown of white hair. But her figure seemed youthful and her gait was far too lively to come from someone suffering her declining years. She was Hinzwala'amaka, a rare Hinzwalan mage whose lifespan bridged through new magic Turns. She could be one hundred years old, Shadow considered – or more if she had lived through a few Turns. Shadow found her appearance in this valley shocking. He knew the names of every Hinzwalan alive, and there were no living Hinzwala'amaka anywhere remotely near here. Even a shy, backward young man like Shadow would be well aware of a woman like this, a woman who was old while still young, a woman who looked and acted like a youth, a girl with white hair. She would be the talk of every child. She would be legend. This one wasn't. And yet, there she was, walking several hundred paces away. Shadow strained his eyes but remained unable to discern her face well enough to sketch a silhouette of her features. A fleeting moment of good lighting suggested a slender nose and lips but it passed too swiftly for Shadow to memorize her visage.

The light *did* expose the colors of her decorative beading and that solidified Shadow's suspicions. She wore the colors of a young, single woman: violets, blues, and oranges. Despite her old age, this woman was no longer bonded to anyone. She'd probably been married once and her husband had died. Then, after seven years had passed, she would have been required to wear the colors of a single woman. Hinzwala'amaka were expected to take a second spouse, to bear another generation of gifted children and to teach them higher forms of magery. This woman was thin. It had probably been years since she'd born any child. She would be expected to fulfill this communal obligation soon.

Curiosity and speculation flashed through Shadow's mind as he watched this woman slowly pacing the valley. Her arms stretched downward toward the earth and her hands held a position suggesting she was petting the air, assuring the ground below she meant it no harm. Her movements and countenance were those of someone gentle, loving, peaceful. Yet, as she moved, Shadow felt the forebodings deepen. His heart swelled with fear and he trembled again. A short eternity passed before he mastered his emotions and calmed his body. In response, the earth shuddered as if she too feared something, as if she knew the future and dreaded what it might bring. Shadow chided himself. Of course the earth feared nothing. She controlled every destiny, didn't she?

As he resolved to jettison such superstitious concerns, Shadow felt the earth tremble with greater fervor. The two men below exchanged knowing glances and then fastened their eyes upon the Hinzwala'amakan woman with more dogged determination. Her petting hands began making erratic clawing motions as if she was grabbing something in the air and throwing it away. In answer, huge clods of dirt flew through the air like splashing water, slowly forming a large earthen ridge that circumscribed the valley. The two men stood motionless, in some odd stance that Shadow thought he recognized from a famous statue in a neighboring village. This was a Hinzwalan brace, a position held when engaging in intense collaborative magery, magic so intense that one had to consciously hold one's feet to the ground. Soon, the ground around the Hinzwala'amakan woman lay bare, naked of any grasses, roots, or shrubbery. Exposed to her power, the earth continued to tremble in distress. Shadow could discern that much now. He dug his fingers deep into the moss covered ground, intuitively summoning courage to fulfill his calling to witness this event.

Even as he braced himself, he considered the obvious: if the earth feared what this woman would do, he should be terrified. Somehow, he mastered his feelings and continued to lie motionless. It would be foolish to expose his position. Besides, he reiterated to himself, whatever evil this woman might bring, whatever demons he might see and wish to forget, he would hold his ground and bear witness.

Larger clods of red earth, bronze sand, and shattering shale rocks flew through the air as if attacking some unseen foe. The mixture of materials the Hinzwala'akan woman dug up seemed unnatural to Shadow. Could they really be naturally mixed like that? But then, what did he know? He was a simple man, barely out of his youth. He farmed his own garden but he never dug this deeply. Anything could be beneath the earth when one dug that far down. Perhaps a long slab of precious metal lay below. Perhaps this Hinzwala'akan woman was unburying some great treasure worthy of every Trayki's dream.

The earth's foreboding grew yet again and soon, towering stripes of ivory were exposed and then gargantuan bones were unveiled. Instead of large clods of bronze earth and shattering boulders mixed with sand, the unearthing became a torrential storm of finer granules. But as the pit grew deeper, the uncovered bronze sand turned ruddy until it resembled some crimson grave where the sand had absorbed the blood of some massive monster. Shadow convulsed involuntarily and then forced himself to master his fear as the beasts' forms emerged. At first, he thought them dracoliches as their ivory bones began pulling together and taking form but after a few moments, he recognized their shapes more clearly. Four wings, four rows of teeth, and a long tail whose tip spread like the three feathers of an arrow. Worse than dracoliches, these were kotrakoy, the cursed beasts of Ali'ikiswan. Only two were uncovered but Shadow knew there was another just outside his view. Desolation was upon the land and he'd been there to witness it.

Slowly, Shadow backed away from the ledge. As he did, one kotrakoy lifted itself high on its legs so that he could see it well. He watched as sinews attached to bone, as muscles formed upon its neck, and as eyes began to form. He watched in horror as the beast slowly regained its grayish-brown reptilian skin and some few modified, decorative feathers that distinguished kotrakoy from other beasts flying around Hiwalani wilds.

Shadow had seen caricatures in children's books and paintings by some of the great masters in the great halls but none of that prepared him for what he saw now. Sitting upright, the largest kotrakoy stood nearly as tall as two homes stacked one on top of another. It's size wasn't what he found so intimidating. It was how it gradually disappeared after it formed. This legendary camouflage had spawned widespread fear of kotrakoy. As long as it remained still, Shadow couldn't even discern its presence, despite the fact he knew precisely where it stood.

He stared at it intently, trying to discern any portion of its newly formed body. He sat in awe, witnessing what no one in his or his father's generation had seen. His eyes were upon the most feared beast in Hiwalani history. He saw a blur as the beast turned its head. Briefly, Shadow looked directly into the eyes of kotrakoy and it looked directly back at him but he only saw those piercing eyes for the slightest of moments before they disappeared once more, fading into the background as impossible camouflage concealed it from all view. Somehow, Shadow considered, it seemed unnatural, even unholy for such an enormous predator to boast such an advantage.

As Shadow turned and considered running away, he experienced the beast's other unfair advantage. He felt the kotrakoy peering into his mind. *It's true. They can read minds,* he intuited. Strangely, Shadow could peer into the kotrakoy's mind as well. He could sense its excitement. He sensed its unique intelligence. He sensed it wouldn't tell the Hinzwalan mages it had seen him because it was too excited to be released from its earthly prison to care about Shadow's trek through its own mind. He raced through some of the beast's memories before those forebodings evolved again, overtook his consciousness. They felt different this time but he couldn't clearly discern the distinction.

Shadow could have taken comfort from his glimpse into the beast's mind. He could have pondered over these details as he casually strolled home, taking care to nurse his blistering feet. He could have pondered the earth's purpose in calling him to witness this horrific development in the land. He could have wondered what he was supposed to do about it.

He didn't.

He ran.

And he took no care of his tender feet. He just let them fly as fast as they could move and resolved himself that he wouldn't stop until he'd warned the Hinzwalan council. He was keenly aware that they probably wouldn't believe him. Perhaps no one would, but he had to try. That was the earth's calling to him. If he understood nothing else, that much was clear. He'd warn everyone what dark magic was upon the land, and if no one else believed him, at least he might save his family from destruction.

Racing to the Village
Some People Don't Just Stare Death
in the Eye and Quickly Recover

Raz'oolenay wasn't unlike other Hiwalani mages. Athletic, medium of build, and average in features, he boasted skin, hair, and eye colors that echoed rich soils native to the area. His soft appearance bespoke his lineage among a people who prided themselves in being one with the earth. What set him apart wasn't any particular physical feature, it was his inability to prove that oneness by summoning the earth's energies to perform even trivial feats of magic. If anything else distinguished Raz'oolenay from his peers, it must have been his long hair. Pleasant in appearance mostly because he smiled frequently, he simply wasn't remarkable in any way.

However, like kotrakoy, he sported his own version of camouflage. Known to disappear into the edges of social gatherings, he could effectively remain unnoticed by anyone, all while carefully observing his ever-changing surroundings. Shying away from attention had earned him the nickname Shadow. And today, for the first time in his life, he felt like he was living up to it, albeit for a new reason. Today he was running from one dark area of the forest to another, carelessly venturing over uneven terrain, hopping over large buttress roots, and consciously ignoring protests from his scorched feet. Today he stayed in the shadows to save his own hide. And he didn't miss the irony of his situation.

Somewhere in his heart, Shadow knew he was needlessly fearful. He knew no kotrakoy were following him. He'd felt their ambition. He knew that overshadowed any interest in the lone azh'nahn who watched them escape their prison and he knew they felt little loyalty to their liberator. Nevertheless, Shadow couldn't govern his feelings. Some people don't just stare death in the eyes and quickly recover. Some people get scared and stay that way. Today Shadow was that kind of person. Today he was hiding.

Running as fast as his fatigued body could handle, Shadow took care not to look at his feet. He'd noticed blisters coming and going. He'd felt that sickening feeling when skin begins to slide and burn and he'd winced when he'd accidentally spotted blood while vaulting over a particularly large Banzna root. Not looking at them wouldn't help them feel better but somehow, averting his eyes helped him worry less.

As he lost himself in the pointless footrace, Shadow pondered last week's training session. Calling him something less than a disappointing failure might have been overstating the case but he'd failed to ignite a fire any child could have started several suns past. He'd resorted to kindling dry leaves with a bow. His father had been so embarrassed that Shadow had expected a first-rate lashing. Instead, he hadn't heard his father's voice for a handful of suns. Shadow probably deserved that. Siring a powerless mage brought deep shame to Hiwalani families. Azh'nahn were considered little more than distant relatives of Trayki and brought into question the value of the entire family.

Some Hiwalani believed villages were better off without such a flawed bloodline among them. Possible suitors of Shadow's sisters would choose to never show any interest. Young women would refuse to associate with his younger brother, limiting his opportunities to marry. At least his older siblings had married already. But Shadow couldn't overlook the repercussions of his failures upon the rest of the family. True enough, the archives bore record that azh'nahn relatives commonly remained among the Hiwalani. However, a few felt a duty to preserve family honor by leaving their homes and village. Demands for their exile would inevitably come, although none would be taken seriously if Shadow took preemptive action. If he thought about anyone besides himself, there was only one meaningful choice: exile. It was the honorable thing to do.

He considered changing course. Perhaps it was best not to return. If his people already believed him self exiled, they'd be disappointed to see him, especially if he bore bad news. And perhaps he would be bearing *old* news. Kotrakoy would arrive before him if they flew toward Hiwalani villages. They may have already raided the outer rim of homes - perhaps an entire village had been decimated by now. On the other hand, if kotrakoy had flown a different direction, his people would be grateful for the opportunity to prepare themselves for the inevitable attack.

His mind raced back to the Hinzwala'amakan mage. Why would she risk kotrakoy raids on her own people? Surely she didn't believe she could control them. Ali'ikiswan hadn't been able to keep control of them with a small host of mages bracing themselves along his side. Sure, he controlled them for a time but ultimately, only burial fully tamed the beasts. It seemed prodigiously prideful for anyone to aspire to greater power than Ali'ikiswan, especially with only two Hinzwala'amakan mages for support.

It seemed an eternity before he arrived at the stream where he had so carelessly fallen before. Despite his foolishness, he was nearly as grateful to find it this second time. Continually scanning the area for anything that might prove dangerous, Shadow worked his way through the darkest corners of the densely covered forest until he found a remote bank where he could refill his flagon and drink all his stomach could hold. Climbing down steep terrain to reach the water was especially painful to his feet but he knew it would be worth it. His mouth was so dry, so sticky and uncomfortable, he worried it would be hard to swallow. As he knelt down and bent over the water, he cupped his hands and began sipping. Every tiny droplet brought welcomed relief.

There, in the dark recesses of the woods, he heard more than he saw images flashing through his mind. The kotrakoy were seeking something. They yearned for communication with people. Their shrieking voices seemed to pierce the air all around him. They scanned the area for anyone who would listen.

Shadow heard them well.

Not only could he see what they were seeing, he could feel their feelings, he could sense their desires. Despite his innate fear of the beasts, he yearned to search their minds, to learn their history. He felt as if he could know whatever they knew but even as he thought this, he sensed kotrakoy shifting their awareness, psyonically reaching toward him. It seemed they wanted to speak to him. Part of him wanted to speak to them as well but he was too terrified to consider the option.

Shadow panicked. Maybe they wanted him after all. Maybe they needed to eliminate any evidence of their presence. Maybe their reappearance was intended to be secret for a time. If so, that strong desire to communicate with him could be nothing more than a manifestation of their desire to kill him. Perhaps Shadow would see those four rows of teeth up close. He shuddered.

He remembered the legends well. Kotrakoy had been bred and magically enhanced to become the ultimate spies, to stop Trayki flying machines from invading Hiwalani lands. With flight, impenetrable camouflage, and the ability to read minds, kotrakoy had been the most ingenious production of Hinzwalan magic in recorded history. Sadly, they had become independent-minded, untrustworthy, and unpredictable. Only the genius of Ali'ikiswan had been able to put them to rest. Rumor claimed he was still alive but if it was true, he would be uncommonly old and unable to put kotrakoy back in their graves. Without his help, Shadow didn't even want to imagine what horror might be upon the land. What fool had done this?

Who was that Hinzwala'amakan woman?

Shadow felt the beasts pressing more intently into the edges of his mind. He was uncertain now: they were trying to locate him, track him down. He shivered again but quickly governed his fears and focused heavily on the soil next to him. Looking for the most nondescript spot he could think of, he glared at the ground as if it was the only thing in life that mattered. He told himself this piece of earth was the most important thing he could imagine, that nothing else mattered. He tried to memorize the position of every pebble, every speck, and every tiny splotch of oddly colored soil. He repeated in his mind the importance of this little plot of land. Shadow sensed the kotrakoy peering into his mind with confusion. He willed that confusion to increase, hoped with every reservoir of energy that their confusion would lead them to leave him alone. For several moments, they continued to waft over his mind, searching for something more concrete to identify his location than a small patch of nondescript soil.

Soon, something distracted them and they gave up. An overwhelming surge of relief passed over Shadow. He desperately wanted to see if he could discern their thoughts to determine *their* destination but a renewed, debilitating fear kept him staring at the ground until he was certain they were far gone.

When it was over and his mind cleared, he noticed he hadn't felt any foreboding. He'd clearly felt fear, but no foreboding. Why would the earth make him heavily dread the unearthing of kotrakoy but leave him without any such feeling when those same beasts sought his life? It made no sense.

Then, one of those impulsive promptings returned. He needed to hurry home. The earth willed him there but he sensed she would pull him slightly off course. Shadow would have been happy to be pulled even farther off course but it seemed he would still pass through Ahz'leniki. *Zhak*, he cursed. Resolved to whatever fate might lie before him, Shadow moved toward the stream, cupped his hands, and drank until he could drink no more. He filled his flagon. Burning sands, several hours of shadeless heat, and little to no water would be the next stage of his test. Shadow took another sip. He needed to be as full of water as his body would allow before running over those sands. If the earth was merciful, his side wouldn't ache.

As hours passed, Shadow pondered his ability to see and feel kotrakoy thoughts. Sure, it had been limited, and it might have been a side-effect of their own search through his mind. Still, it was something. It was a small success in an *advanced* form of magery. Few ever mastered telepathy. At a time when his life as an epic failure had been mounting like a pile of rocks at the bottom of an avalanche, this was an unusual and noteworthy success. The contradiction glowered at him like a hungry predator. Perhaps it was a fluke. Perhaps it was part of his test. Or, maybe it was nothing more than a display of kotrakoy power: perhaps it deliberately opened its mind to him. That seemed more probable.

But why?

Because he was Ahz'nahn, Shadow doubted anyone would believe this part of his story. He determined he wouldn't tell anyone these details. For now, he would simply ponder these things and wonder what purpose the earth had in choosing him as witness for this event, the event that would change the course of history, the event that would define his generation.

Hours passed. Sands changed into shaded woodlands not far from home. His muscles protested and refused to go any farther. The continual pressure of the promptings all but disappeared. He could rest now. He had been following Izhnat, a large tributary that bordered a block of neighboring villages. Perhaps kotrakoy would first attack Hiwalani villages on this side of the mountains. That would explain his path.

That was it, he decided. They be warned first. Whatever the reason, he was grateful for a reprieve from the breakneck speed he had been traveling. With uncommon stiffness, Shadow sat down to rest his feet in the cool and shadowy waters of Izhnat. He knew better but he didn't take off his sandals. They would last longer if they were not regularly drenched in water. He'd been taught that since toddlerhood but he was too exhausted to care. Besides, the water would wash away those pesky granules of sand that chaffed the bottoms of his feet.

After a few moments, the waters seemed to grow colder and Shadow felt chilled but he was too tired to move, too tired to care. He fell to one side, curled his legs so that his feet mostly left the water, and gratefully gave up consciousness.

SHADOW AWAKENED TO A CRASHING SOUND unlike anything he'd heard before, except when felling trees for building projects. No one would be harvesting trees here. Felling Eznaki trees with towering buttress roots was far too difficult to make it worthwhile. The noise had to be something else. Confused, Shadow found himself squinting through violent shards of light piercing the canopy. As he walked toward the sound, it returned - that familiar, impulsive prompting. Perhaps he was being called to witness another event. He hoped it wasn't kotrakoy. He begged the earth not to require him to see kotrakoy up close. Nothing could be more horrifying.

He took a resolute breath and winced. From the waist down, he felt like he'd finished running a thousand festival courses. A decent runner, Shadow always enjoyed festival races but he never got conditioned enough to prevent that horrible burning sensation that comes after you've run harder than normal. Today seemed worse than ever. More than three days of nearly nonstop trekking seemed harder than festival racing. He winced with nearly every footstep as he made his way toward the source of the ominous crashing sound. There were no further noises, nothing other than feelings to help him discern where he was going. Wherever it was, it couldn't be too far.

Soon, he came upon a darkly veiled patch of trees where a young Trayki woman slowly swayed back and forth, hanging upside down with her leg attached to some strange Trayki rope. She looked like some discombobulated pendulum. He traced the rope upward to its source where a brightly colored flying contraption rested in multiple contortions among the treetops. *That is why we were never meant to fly,* Shadow impulsively repeated in his mind. Flying machines had brought war upon Hiwalani a few generations past. Flying machines had inspired Hinzwalan elite to breed and create the kotrakoy. The contraptions were unnatural, unholy.

An occasional drop of blood traced its way through the woman's blonde hair and splatted upon the ground. Part of Shadow wanted to see her up close. Part of him thought he should leave the scene to ponder why he'd been called to witness the death of this flying enemy. Curiosity won the battle. Shadow's eyes traced the rope, following it to the largest branch it hung from and then to the trunk he would need to climb to cut the blonde woman down.

Without thinking, Shadow removed his sandals at the base of the tree and began climbing. Blistered and worn feet objected to the scratchy bark but he refused to focus on the unpleasant sensations. *It's best not to give pain attention.* That's what his father always said. Having never carefully considered the advice, Shadow followed it instinctively, and it helped. Soon, he was crawling along the branch where the Trayki rope held the blonde captive.

By the time he reached the spot, Shadow had a plan as to how he would dislodge the rope from around the branch without sending the young woman crashing the remaining distance to the ground. A stretch of the rope above wound around a few small branches that would afford some extra length. Because the rope was lodged between a fork in the branch he was on, Shadow estimated that by cutting it next to the branches above while pulling it toward the tree, he would be able to gently lower the blonde to the ground, or at least lower her close enough that the remaining fall would be relatively mild. Carefully, he pulled a black blade out of its sheath, tightly grabbed the rope, tugged it towards the tree trunk until it was snug against the fork of the branch, and cut the rope with his other hand.

It didn't work.

The jolt from the cut jolted the rope harder than Shadow expected and left him gasping as he lost his grip. The rope whizzed against the forked branches until its tip ripped past the branch altogether. An instant later, a heavy thud left Shadow assuming that if this stranger woman hadn't been dead before, she certainly must be now. Her neck would be broken.

Shadow winced. He'd assumed she was already dead but the possibility that she might have been alive left him cringing with shame. Mistreatment of a corpse was unnecessary and dishonorable. Mistreatment of an innocent person was unthinkable to a man of honor. Even Trayki deserved better. Shadow was grateful no one else had seen it. Still, good intentions rarely soothe guilt. His heart sank as he considered the ill treatment he'd given the blonde woman, whether or not she'd been dead before the fall.

Slowly, he slunk down the tree branch and its trunk like some animal scolded by its master. Unwilling to look at the young woman now, he focused on gently replacing his sandals before standing up. His eyes traced the ground and refused to gaze upon the corpse. Feelings of mortification and humiliation welled up inside and refused to be quashed. True enough, no one would ever know what happened. But he would know and the earth would know and that was too much.

When his peripheral vision spotted the blonde, Shadow finally allowed his eyes to observe her condition. *Too many clothes,* he considered. Trayki were odd that way. This one had loose-fitting clothes that covered nearly everything but her face. Even her sandals wrapped entirely around her feet until they couldn't be seen at all. Shadow wondered how anyone could live with so many things tied around one's body. Surely, all of these clothes restricted motion, restricted one's ability to feel the earth's renewing energy.

He considered another possibility. Maybe Trayki clothes were meant to direct attention to their hair. This one had beautiful hair, apart from splotches of crimson. He stared at her hair for a moment before adjusting her body into a less contorted position. He considered cutting some of her golden locks. If woven, it would make an exquisite bookmark, he thought. But of course, he couldn't really do that. It would be sacrilege to the body.

Emotions overran Shadow once again. He could feel the earth prompting him toward the blonde. He needed to turn her over. It was almost as if the earth wanted to punish him for what he'd done, to castigate him for being careless. She now required him to see the blonde's face before burying her. *How should I do it?* He considered wrapping her in more cloth and leaving her in the trees. That's how they did it during the Trayki war. *Is that their custom?* Shadow wondered for the first time.

With so much clothing, Shadow considered that maybe he should have just left her hanging. Maybe that wasn't disrespectful in her culture. He considered the possibility. Trayki were backward people. They liked to fly. Perhaps they preferred burial in the trees. It seemed uncivilized but so did a great many other Trayki customs. Probably, he should have left her hanging and moved on. If that was Trayki custom, perhaps the earth herself had buried this young woman. Maybe her face had been left uncovered to shame her for riding in a flying contraption, a punishment for her unnatural curiosity and desires. But then, why had he been called here?

Eyes fixated upon her gorgeous golden locks, Shadow carefully placed his thumb along the top side of her neck and cupped the remaining portion of his hand around the base of her skull. Then, he rotated her head as he rolled her body to keep the corpse from bending in unnatural contortions. Trayki or not, she should be treated with respect. If he failed in this duty, someone might not honorably dispose of his body when he died. As her face came into view, Shadow forced back tears. He'd never seen a Trayki before. He'd seen pictures of their men in history books and he'd easily identified this one because of her hair but seeing her up close was unnerving, and surprising.

Her visage was pristine, delicate, stunning. Shadow governed rekindled, feelings of mourning as he brushed aside her long, matted hair and remarked again how he'd never seen anything quite so breathtaking as her unusual hair. Even rustic monkey hair was not this exquisite, shiny. These golden locks nearly glowed when the sun warmed them.

Hiwalani custom all but demanded song in the presence of surprising beauty but Shadow couldn't bring himself to sing for shame of how he'd already dishonored her. He managed to muster an intermittent hum but it was too solemn for its intended purpose.

As he made note of that thought, he considered something new. Perhaps Trayki bodies were horrifically ugly. Perhaps that was why this one was so heavily covered. He traced his hand along her body as he adjusted it into lying position. It seemed normal. Perhaps ugly texture or splotchy coloring contaminated the skin.

As he contemplated that possibility, the blonde Trayki drew in air as she haphazardly swung her arm toward his face. Shadow instinctively recoiled, avoided the attack as quickly as she fell back into the oblivion of unconsciousness. As alarmed as he was that she was alive, he was equally surprised that she feared him. He supposed that was natural in enemy territory but having no intention to harm or dishonor her, he wouldn't have imagined the possibility moments before, even if she'd been fully awake. He gently stroked her cheeks to assuage her fear, uncertain if she was mildly aware of his presence or completely incapacitated.

Perhaps she was suffering, wishing she were dead, wishing the pain would end. Hiwalani tradition required someone's permission before ending their pain. His heart sank once more.

He didn't speak Trayki and he was no healer. He was barely capable of bandaging a moderate wound, let alone taking care of a woman with a broken neck and bloody head injuries. He wished he wasn't there, wished he hadn't followed the earth's call, wished he hadn't cut the line, wished …

Shadow nudged the woman's head slightly sideways and pushed aside her hair until he could see the underlying cuts. Only afterward did he consider that maybe he shouldn't be moving her neck like that, especially if it was broken, but it was too late now. He grabbed a nearby branch that had fallen next to the body, placed it under her neck for support, and inspected the wound. It wasn't nearly as bad as he expected but it was still bleeding a slow, steady stream. She continued to breathe.

Shadow again unsheathed his blade and began cutting long strips of cloth out of the strange clothes covering her belly. He wondered again how unnatural her skin might look. If she survived, she might feel ashamed by the unsightly exposure of her deformed skin. He frowned as he considered the possibility but when he cut the material and removed it, it exposed normal, if not bronze, skin. There seemed no reason to hide it. It was beautiful like her face.

Pondering this new discovery, Shadow carefully wrapped the cloth strip around her head and wished he knew how to stitch a wound or bind it back together with magic. He couldn't blame himself for not having mastered the healing arts. Few did, but he regretted it nonetheless. Self deprecation had become a habit. It was one thing he'd really mastered. He was azh'nahn; he deserved it. That didn't stop him from feeling pangs of disappointment that he couldn't serve her better. He hated feeling useless. He'd never get used to that.

In a flash, the blonde flicked her eyes open, as if searching for something in the canopy above. Frightened, they saw nothing but forest and a mangled glider. Her eyes were a mysterious bluish hue, unlike anything Shadow had seen except perhaps on azh'malam blossoms from Ireenla.

Shadow only observed them for a moment before they sagged shut. Still, in that moment, he saw into her soul. Athna. Born third into a family of seven, she had a happy childhood. She was adventurous. She loved the outdoors. She loved to study and to dance and to sculpt. And she loved to fly.

Shadow saw through her mind the moment she'd crashed. He felt her fear, her surprise. He felt her loosen her feet from the pedals that powered the flying contraption. He felt her concern that she might never see her family again, her concern that Hiwalani might torture and kill her, that she might have started a war by crashing in this forbidden land. He felt her love and concern for her family. And having felt all that, Shadow couldn't help but love her as well.

Although he'd never felt it before, he recognized another feeling: hal'eeyeeka, the soul bond. It felt like a long wash of energy enveloping his soul, cleansing him from all the wrongs he'd ever committed and bonding him to this stranger as if their souls had always been one. It was a sacred pairing by the earth herself. Athna would have to choose him before the bond was complete but until then, Shadow was bound as her protector.

The thought made him shudder. Azh'nahn as protectorate. The idea was laughable. Still, few would take the responsibility more seriously than he did and none would be as devout.

As he memorized her pristine visage, Shadow gently traced his fingers along her neck. He tried not to press hard but firmly enough to feel her vertebrae. As far as he could tell, they all felt intact and she didn't wince when he touched them. Maybe that was because she was out cold. Maybe her senses were gone and she would die soon. Either way, Shadow didn't know what to do and feeling no prompting to guide him, he kept an eye on the bandage to make sure the bleeding had stopped. He squeezed up and down her arms and legs, hands and feet, to verify whether or not she had broken anything. Visible injuries seemed insignificant. He imagined internal injuries were worse, hoped she'd heal.

Intuitively, a profound concern for her health welled inside, perhaps magnified by the soul bond, perhaps not. Shadow naturally yearned to serve others. He'd been raised that way. Regardless, the desire was manifesting itself unusually strongly and he intended to do everything he could to nurse Athna back to health.

Hours passed. To Shadow's surprise, she barely stirred all day. Only her breathing proved she wasn't dead. He didn't think her wound seemed so bad, and he'd bandaged it well, but she slept soundly nonetheless.

Throughout the day, Shadow gathered various roots and made small meals while keeping an eye upon the mysterious blonde. Several times, he pondered how he'd seen into her mind, how he'd felt her feelings. *Just like kotrakoy.* Only this time, there was nothing to explain how it had happened. It left him exhilarated. He felt a germ of increasing confidence, a tinge of hope for his future.

He wished he could hear her voice. Perhaps, in the morning, she would wake and speak with him.

Then, he felt dumb. Even if she spoke to him, he realized, her words would be Trayki gibberish. Then again, perhaps he could speak to her in pictures. Perhaps she could see things in his mind as he showed them to her. Silently, he castigated himself for such foolishness. A splinter of success couldn't justify such delusional hope. These things take time.

When nightfall descended, his thoughts fell into the fog of sleep. He successfully ignored fears that he might not return in time to warn his people about the impending danger. He trusted the earth's judgment.

As he dreamed, that trust dissipated. He dreamed of decimation, of dwindling Hiwalani strength. He dreamed of hopelessness. He saw Hiwalani relying upon him and becoming angry when he had nothing to offer. His duty had been to expose the Hinzwala'amakan's deed and nothing more. All was lost and he was to blame. These and worse things he dreamed. But he never left Athna's side. He lay down upon the earth's lap with his head firm against Athna's left arm. If she moved, he would wake up.

Made in the USA
San Bernardino, CA
26 May 2018